TIME of the WITCHES

Also by Anna Myers

Red-Dirt Jessie
Rosie's Tiger
Graveyard Girl
Spotting the Leopard
The Keeping Room
Fire in the Hills
Ethan Between Us
Captain's Command
When the Bough Breaks
Stolen by the Sea
Tulsa Burning
Flying Blind
Hoggee
Assassin
Confessions from the Principal's Chair
Wart
Spy!

TIME of the WITCHES

Anna Myers

Walker & Company  New York

First published in the United States of America in 2009 by
Walker Publishing Company, Inc.
Visit Walker & Company's Web site at www.walkeryoungreaders.com

For information about permission to reproduce selections from this book, write to Permissions, Walker & Company, 175 Fifth Avenue, New York, New York 10010

Library of Congress Cataloging-in-Publication Data
Myers, Anna.
Time of the witches / Anna Myers.
p. cm.
Summary: Orphaned Drucilla finds a home with the beautiful but troubled Mistress Putnam as accusations of witchcraft start to swirl in Salem Village.
ISBN-13: 978-0-8027-9820-6 • ISBN-10: 0-8027-9820-9
[1. Witchcraft—Fiction. 2. Trials (Witchcraft)—Fiction. 3. Salem (Mass.)—History—Colonial period, ca. 1600–1775—Fiction. 4. Orphans—Fiction.] I. Title.
PZ7.M9814Ti 2009 [Fic]—dc22 2008054278

Book design by Danielle Delaney
Typeset by Westchester Book Composition
Printed in the U.S.A. by Quebecor World Fairfield
2 4 6 8 10 9 7 5 3 1

All papers used by Walker & Company are natural, recyclable products made from wood grown in well-managed forests. The manufacturing processes conform to the environmental regulations of the country of origin.

To Samuel Benjamin Bluejacket Lane

Sweet baby Sam, you are exactly one month old on the day I write this page. You are forty-five miles away from me, and it is hard for me to stay here and work instead of going to rock you. You have been given two middle names because your parents wanted to name you Benjamin after your mother's brother and Bluejacket after the maiden name of your father's mother.

I don't know yet who you will look like, but I know you are lucky to have the mother, father, and big brother that you have. I know, too, that all of us are blessed to have you. I hope you will grow up to have your father's intelligence, his interest in learning new things, and his sense of loyalty. I also hope you will have your mother's tender heart and her quickness to love. You are my fifth grandchild, but there has been an exclusive place in my heart saved just for you. Thank you for giving me one of your special first smiles. Welcome to our world, Sammy. We have all been waiting for you.

TIME of the WITCHES

PART ONE

The Early Years

Chapter One

We were born at the exact same time, Gabe and I. It was that hour just before dawn when the cock first crows to the world that day is coming. Was it of a certain, then? Did the timing of our births mean our spirits came into the world united? Who can say? I know only that nothing separated our hearts, not until we were fifteen, not until those darkest of days, not until the time of the witches.

The midwife, Goody Curry, has told me the story of our births, told me how she brought our mothers together. "Load one of them up and move her to the other, else I won't see to neither," she said to our white-faced fathers who had come almost at the same time to fetch her in the middle of a January night, bitter with cold. She folded her arms in front of her. "You decide or else you can birth your own babies, that's what." She made a shooing motion with her hands. "Outside with you. Settle it there. Makes me no never mind which house." She reached for a half-empty bottle of oil that wanted filling considering two pairs of eyes would need to be cleansed.

Our mothers were young and afraid. Their acquaintance with each other had been but slight, my mother having come to Salem Village just a year before as a bride. Still each was happy for the company of the other. As the hours passed and the pain increased, a bond grew between them. "My baby," gasped the fair-haired woman between groans, "promise me you will suckle my baby should I die."

From across the room the dark-haired woman managed a laugh. "You won't die," she said. "We will barely remember this agony on the morrow. That's what they say, anyway."

"But promise me. Henry couldn't care for a newborn."

"I promise," said the other.

"Hush! There will be no talk of dying," thundered the midwife. "I've not lost a woman this year." She wiped the fair-haired woman's brow. No one spoke of the fact that the year was only three weeks old.

"Surely by God's mercy, they won't come at the same time," the midwife muttered to the daughter she had dragged from bed to assist her, but they did, a boy, Gabe, for the fair-haired woman and a girl, me, for the dark-haired one.

"Ma," said the midwife's daughter when the baby slipped out into her hands, "it's a boy. Oh, Ma, ain't he grand?" She had never before attended a birth. She held the wet infant up for his mother to see.

"Cut the cord," said the midwife. "Mind what I do and follow just so." In minutes both of us were wrapped in soft material and laid beside our mothers. The fair-haired mother spoke gentle words of love to her baby boy and traced his small face with her finger. The dark-haired mother's eyes were closed.

"The bleeding," cried the midwife to her daughter. "The bleeding's not right! Quick, child, soak more cloth for compresses, hurry!"

Alarmed, the fair-haired woman raised herself on her elbow. "Jayne," she called. "Jayne, are you all right?"

No answer came from the quiet form. The midwife went to

the head of the bed, placed her hand on the woman's heart, and leaned close to her face. "There's breath, but little."

Our fathers, who had not yet been called into the room, burst through the door, each to the bedside of his wife. My father, Matthew Overbey, dropped to his knees, burying his face in the bedclothes. "Don't die, Jayne, oh please don't die."

At just that moment, I've been told, I began to wail, a feeble sound, but one that still managed to fill the room. "Henry, bring her to me," the fair-haired woman told her husband.

He raised his huge hands to study them. "Pick it up? I'd not know how, Mary."

She reached to prod at his side. "You'd best put your mind to learning."

Stepping around my father, Henry Matson scooped up the crying baby and carried me with shaking hands to his wife, who placed my small body beside the other one. The baby girl stopped crying. "She finds comfort in him," Mary whispered to her husband. " 'Tis well for I fear it is us who will be about raising her."

My mother, Jayne Overbey, who had been carried into the Matson's house by her husband, was also carried from it to be put into a wooden box and buried in the nearby cemetery. He was, the midwife told me, a broken man who looked but once at his baby girl.

"I'll keep her if that's your wish," said Mary Matson. "Jayne promised me she'd feed my babe if I died. I'll gladly do for hers."

"Until she's older," my father said, and he touched me once on my forehead. He moved quickly then toward the door.

"Wait," called Mary. "What of a name? What is she to be called?"

He did not turn back. "Drucilla," he said softly. "Jayne picked Drucilla for a girl."

We grew together, always together. The baby boy was named Gabriel, and his first word was "Dru."

The next part of my story is wispy. Can it be that I have memory from that time? I seem to, seem to be able to close my eyes and see us, two babes together. Mayhap, it is only a recollection of an oft-heard story. Either way, there is in my mind an image of that day when my father came for me. He had not often visited his little girl, but now he had a new wife. It was time, he declared, that he took his daughter home.

"She's so like Jayne," he said, and he bent down to reach for me.

I pulled away from his touch. Gabriel moved quickly to my side. "My Dru," he said, and we wrapped our small arms around each other tightly.

"Come, child," Matthew said, and he held out his arms. "I'm your father, and I want to take you home."

Mary reached for Gabriel and Matthew for me. They pried our little bodies apart, both of us wailing and struggling to reach the other.

"Could you leave her," said Mary, "but for a time, yet? Until she's old enough to understand that she belongs to you."

He did, but before Matthew Overbey could come back for his daughter, death came for him. He was killed when a big limb he was chopping from a tree swung the unexpected way and struck him full in the head. Oft I have wondered if things might have been different had even one of my parents lived. Surely, then, I would not have been filled always with that aching yearning to belong.

Death was a regular visitor in the forlorn village of Salem, and he came for Mary and Henry Matson, too, during a smallpox epidemic when we were around four. Now Gabe and I truly had only each other. "Keep them together," Mary pleaded with her last breath. "Please keep the wee ones together."

The good people of Salem Village did keep us together, first one neighbor then another taking us in and sharing what were, at times, provisions hard come-by. To their credit, I must state that never were we truly hungry, nor were we mistreated.

Like our mothers, we were exact opposites in coloring. Gabe was fair of skin, his hair soft and like sunshine. I had my mother's thick, dark hair. It hung in ringlets, and Gabe as a small boy pointed out that I had "round hair."

We were different in temperament also. Gabe had a stubborn streak. Even as a little boy, he would set his mouth in determination and knit his brows. I learned early on not to try to push him when I saw that expression. Gabe did not give up. I was more pliable, an easygoing child, likely to be led.

In our sixth year we experienced a horrifying event. We were, at the time, living with a family named Carver, a woman and man who had three boys somewhat older than we were. One cold night a fire began when a piece of unseasoned firewood exploded, sending a burning ember into the room. The main hall was ablaze before anyone woke.

I recall being awakened by the shouting, and I remember feeling the heat coming from the front of the house. "Hurry," I heard one of the Carver boys call, "get out the back door. Don't stop for anything." Gabe and I followed the boys' forms through the smoke. About halfway into the kitchen, I thought of my most precious possession, a miniature portrait of my mother. In the same tiny black velvet bag it came in, it was kept always tucked between my mattress and the rope that supported it.

Saying nothing, I whirled about and began making my way back to the sleeping chamber. I suppose in the smoke no one noticed my going. It was impossible to see anything. I moved by feeling my way, touching the long table first, and then the wall. I struggled with the terrible tightness in my chest that made it difficult to breathe, and the journey seemed a long one. When finally I reached my bed, I dropped to the floor and retrieved the bag, but I did not get back up. I thought I would put my head down to rest for only a moment. Evidently, I had been missed by that time, and I began to hear their voices, faint and far-away sounding. "Dru," I heard Gabe call. There were other voices, too, telling him not to go back into the house. I felt too tired to stand, and I lost interest in the voices. I was asleep when Gabe reached me.

Poking and pulling, he woke me. "Come on!" he shouted. "If we don't hurry, we will die." He gave my arm a mighty jerk. I wanted only to sleep, but he would not leave me be. Coughing, I managed to stand, and he pulled me out of the sleeping chamber, through the kitchen, and out the door where we both collapsed on the snow, me still grasping the velvet bag.

The Carvers all talked about how Gabe had saved my life and said that I had been near dead when he got to me. I was grateful and said a proper thank you to him, but I remember, too, that I said something else. "Gabe," I told him just before we went to sleep that night among hay and farm animals in the Carver's barn. "I found me out something tonight. I found out that dying doesn't seem so bad. In fact, it might be rather pleasant. It makes me feel better, you know, for our parents."

"Drucilla," he muttered, "sometimes you are most strange. Now go to sleep."

The next morning we went to live with a kind woman known to all as Granny Morton. How she came to own a house and to possess provisions enough to share with us, I do not know, for there was no man to work her fields. In fact, we lived rather more comfortably than we ever had before, each of us with our own sleeping chamber. We dwelt with the woman until we were just past ten. What her age really was I have no notion, but she seemed ancient. Her back was bent so that we, even at six, were almost her equal in height. She had white hair that was wound about her head in neat rolls and usually kept beneath a lace cap.

Granny Morton was naught but kind to us. I remember her gentle touch, and the bright, smiling eyes among the wrinkles of her face. Still, I never gave my heart to her. By six, I had learned that only Gabe was permanent in my life, only Gabe should be loved.

It was Granny Morton who taught us to read and write, skills Gabe was quick to acquire. Looking back, it seems as if Gabe needed someone only to hand him a book and to give him permission to read it before becoming a scholar.

I was more slow to learn and remained fairly uninterested in the entire process until the day when Granny said, "You best learn, child. One day the two of you may be separated. When that happens, you will want to send Gabe letters, and to read what he sends back, will you not?"

I had stood and was wandering away from the table where Granny sat between us, an open Bible before her. I remember whirling quickly back to face her. Separated from Gabe? I could see that Granny believed such dire event to be possible. I would learn to read and write.

Those were good years, the ones we spent with Granny. Gabe grew strong enough to chop wood. I learned to make bread, to sew, and to spin flax. Granny owned several books and she even owned a lute, which to my delight she taught me to play. Many an evening we spent near the glow of the fire. Aided with candlelight, Gabe would read to us while Granny and I stayed busy with needles or in kneading bread. Sometimes I plucked the strings of the lute while we sang. "Greensleeves" was my favorite, and I am always transported back to Granny Morton's when I hear the melody.

During our days at Granny's there was time for us to play. Gabe's favorite game was to pretend we were at church. He was, of course, the minister, and I, along with Granny's old dog, made up the congregation. Gabe liked the game much more than I did because he got to do all the talking. I remember a day when I decided I would put an end to his playing at being a preacher. "You could never be a real minister," I told him, and I folded my arms across my chest.

That stubborn look I knew so well came to his face. "I will be a minister," he said. "I've made my mind up to it already."

I shook my head. "No, you are not nearly mean enough. Everyone knows a minister must do a great deal of shouting and pounding his fists while he speaks. You will never do." I stood and walked away. I called Granny's dog to follow me, but he would not because he loved Gabe best.

"See?" Gabe shouted. "Brownie likes my sermons!"

I did not look back. "Brownie is too tired to move!" I yelled. Later, unable to bear the hurt expression he still wore, I told Gabe I was sorry. I added, though, that I did not want to play Sabbath anymore. "It is a dull game," I said.

He sat at the table with one of Granny's books before him. I felt jealous of the way Granny exclaimed over how smart he was, and I felt jealous, too, of the books that took his time away from me. He liked to read aloud to me. Ordinarily, I understood very little of what he read and would sit still for only short passages at a time.

Our happy life with Granny ended all too soon. One snowy day, when we had just passed our tenth birthday, Granny did not get up in the morning. We found her in her bed. Her skin, when we touched her, was cold. Death had come again into our lives. Crying, we stood, huddled together, and looked down on her kind face.

"We have to go to the neighbors," I said after a time. It was but a short walk to Jacob Crown's home, but the snow was too deep for the horse and cart. Gabe used the ax to craft thin sheets of wood that we tied beneath our shoes, making it somewhat easier to walk on the snow. We wrapped blankets over our cloaks, and holding hands we set out.

The Crowns took us in that day, and they kept us for two years. The gentleman who had claim to Granny Morton's property brought Gabe her books, and he gave the lute to me. The Crowns had two boys, twins who were just learning to walk. I worked at minding the babes and learning more about sewing while Gabe helped in the fields. It was while we were with the Crowns that we learned about Gabe's gift with animals. Jacob Crown had accepted a cow as payment for some carpentry work he had done for a person in Salem Town. "I've been cheated!" he bellowed when he came into the kitchen where his wife and I were preparing the evening meal. "Won't even let me touch her, much less stand still for milking." He set his empty wooden pail down hard on the table.

Gabe had just come in from the henhouse with a basket of eggs. "Do you mind if I have a go at it?"

Jacob shook his head. "Don't want you around her. She's that wild."

"I'd like to try." Gabe handed me the eggs. "I'll be careful."

Jacob pointed to the bucket. "Well, then, give it a go, but I'm telling you you're apt to be kicked in the head."

My heart began to race. I had always known that animals

seemed to like Gabe, but none of those creatures had been dangerous. I put the eggs in the cupboard. "Wait! I'm going with you!" I shouted to his back as he went out the door.

"You stop here," Gabe whispered to me when we had opened the barn door. "I don't want her to see you or hear you." He put his finger to his lips, and I made no protest.

He moved slowly into the barn, talking softly as he walked. "There's a good old girl," he said. "No one asked you if you wanted to move, did they? There, there, I know how that feels. Yes, I do." The cow turned her head and looked at him. Gabe reached out to pat her head. He moved slowly along her side, patting and talking softly. "I'd like to milk you now. You don't mind, do you?" Using his foot, he pushed the stool into place. "There's a good old girl." He began to milk. I remember well how I stood in the doorway, watching, and I remember a knowledge coming to me, the knowing that Gabriel Matson was no ordinary boy.

Jacob Crown was a master woodworker and, under his instruction, Gabe began to carve small figures. In no time his work was quite good. He mostly created animals. "The boy is a pure wonder," I heard Jacob tell his wife. "Is there anything he can't do?" The words made me feel proud of Gabe, but I must admit, too, that I felt envy.

Gabe's stubborn pride sometimes got him in trouble. Once while we lived with the Crowns, it almost cost him his life. It was spring, and Gabe and I had been sent to look for huckleberries. At first we separated, and when we met, Gabe was rather put out because my bucket was almost full. "You've done much better than I have," he said.

"You're not much of a berry finder," I said when I saw the few berries at the bottom. Then I noticed a stain about his mouth. "You'd have a deal more, I'd guess, if the ones in your stomach were put in the bucket instead.

He frowned. "Come along," he said. "Let's look for more." We had wandered farther than ever before and came to a deeply gouged creek, cut through rock. A bush laden with berries could be seen across the ravine.

"Well," I said, "you won't get those. There's no climbing down there."

"I could jump over." He moved to the edge and studied the other bank.

I was horrified. "You couldn't," I said quickly. "If you missed, the fall would surely kill you."

He was quiet for a moment, studying the chasm. He set down his bucket. "When I'm over there, I'll take off my jacket and tie the berries in it about my waist," he said.

"Gabe," I said, "please don't. Look at the rocks you'd fall on."

He shook his head. "It's not far. I am certain I could make it."

I took hold of his arm. "Don't do it," I begged, but he pulled free from me and began to back up for a run at it.

Unable to watch, I covered my eyes with my hands, but his scream made me look. I saw his feet moving frantically as he slid off the bank he had only barely reached. He grabbed at a bush that grew near the edge, and his body dangled there with nothing for a foothold in the rock wall. Frantic thoughts flashed through my mind. I had to try the jump, had to try to save him. If I failed, we both would die. If I did not try, I would be left on earth alone, without Gabe. The choice was easy. I whirled about and ran farther back than he had. I took off my skirt and heavy shoes, and I ran as I had never run before, ran toward that bank, praying over and over in my mind. The jump took only a second, and I felt myself land on the opposite bank. In another second, I had rolled to the spot where he dangled. Taking hold of his arm, I pulled with all my might.

"Gabe Matson," I said when he had thrown up his leg and was

able to climb over to be beside me. "I am never going berry picking with you again."

We had to walk quite some distance to find a bridge and then make our way back to collect my things. Before we began, though, Gabe did fill his jacket with berries. I did not help, and I complained mightily about walking with bare feet and in only my shift.

"Very well," Gabe said. He sat down, removed his shoes, and gave them to me. They were too large and made blisters. Still, they were better than no shoes at all. He thanked me over and over for saving him, but never once did he hint that he should not have tried the jump at all. I felt most vexed with him the rest of the day and a good bit of the next.

When we were just past twelve, the Crowns sold everything and prepared to move to Maine. "I'll not be taking the young ones," Jacob Crown told the village selectmen, "but they are strong and glad to do a full day's work." The meeting was in the church building, and Jacob turned his head to the back of the room where he had told us to sit. "I have them with me. Stand up now, Gabriel. You, too, Drucilla. Let these men see how big it is you've grown."

We stood. I remember how my legs shook, and I held to the back of the bench in front of me. "We won't be together," I whispered to Gabe when we were seated again. "No one will take us both."

Gabe shook his head. "Nay, we stay together."

And so word went out to the village that two young people needed positions as servants. Soon we both had to accept the real possibility of being separated. Mary Putnam, widow of old Thomas Putnam, sent word at once that she wanted the boy. Her only son, Joseph, had just taken a wife and built himself a home. She could use Gabe about the house for odd jobs and for company.

Thomas Putnam Jr., Mary's stepson, would take me. "That's good!" I said, jumping from the floor I had been scrubbing when Jacob brought us word. "We go to households of kinsmen. At least we will see each other often."

Jacob Crown laughed. "You know naught about the Putnams. Mary Putnam and her son, Joseph, are hated by his half brothers, who claim that they were cheated by their father's will." He laughed again. "Like as not, Ann Putnam pushed Thomas Junior to speak for you because she thought Mary might decide to take you both. Ann's always wanting whatever Mary might have."

With misery a great ball inside me, I dropped back to the floor and picked up my scrub rag. Gabe came from where he had just put wood on the fire and knelt beside me. "Don't fret, Round Hair," he told me, and he pulled at the dark curl that had slipped from beneath my white cap. "Their farms are side by side. We will find a way to see each other. Let the Putnams fight each other. It is no matter. They can't separate us. You'll see."

PART TWO

The Middle Years

Chapter Two

The misery that had begun inside me grew to the point that I could move only with a great effort, as if I walked through water. Spring and muddy roads had come to Salem Village. I prayed that the carriage would get stuck, but Thomas Putnam urged his horses on through the mire. His face was not unkind, and at first he had tried to talk to me. "My wife is glad you're coming," he had said pleasantly, "and young Ann, why she's apt to swoon from excitement. She's nine and . . ." He paused for a moment. "Well, our little girl needs a friend, she does." I did not comment. Had I tried to speak, the great sob inside me would most surely have escaped.

I hunched low on the carriage bench, partly to shield myself from the wind still sharp with winter's leftovers and partly because I did not have the strength for sitting up. I kept my head turned to the west, searching the horizon. Gabriel was somewhere toward the west. Joseph Putnam had said so when he had come to fetch Gabe for his mother.

Joseph, a sympathetic young man, had been touched by the sorrow with which Gabe and I parted from each other, Gabe's face growing white and me putting my hands over my eyes, unable to look. "You just turn to the west," Joseph had told me, "that's to the left when you're on the main road. On a clear day you will be able to see the smoke from my mother's house. You'll be that close when you're at Thomas's place."

Only when the carriage stopped did I turn my eyes from the west to look at the house. It was a fine place, much larger than any of the homes where I had lived before. A woman came running from the door, followed by a small girl. "There's my wife now," said Thomas, "and our little Ann. Did I not tell you they are excited?"

The carriage stopped. The two now stood looking up at me. The child was lean, too lean to be a girl who lived in such a fine house, where food must be abundant, but she was tall for nine. I supposed that growing tall had made her thin. She was blond and her face would have been pretty had her expression been different. She looked strangely old, tired, and very sad. I doubted the truth of her father's words about her being glad I had come.

The woman, though, was beautiful—with eyes that seemed to have a blue fire to them and hair that looked like plaited gold gathered on top of her head. Even in her plain brown dress, she looked elegant.

"Hello." She held up her hand, took mine, and squeezed it. "I'm Mistress Putnam." She leaned around the carriage to call to her husband. "Thomas, come help Drucilla down." I could not take my gaze from the woman's face. Never had I met a woman who called herself Mistress. All the women I knew were called Goodwife or Goody for short. Mistress was a term reserved for the upper class.

When my feet were on the ground, Mistress Putnam came and took my arm. I saw then that the woman's loose clothing was meant to conceal that she was large with child. Knowing what had happened to my mother, I always feared for women who were soon to face childbirth. This time, though, the fear was worse. I wished that I had not come here to live where a woman might die and where a girl so clearly did not want me about.

The woman, though, was smiling. "Do you like our house?" she asked with a wave of her arm toward the structure, but she did not wait for an answer. "It is, I believe, the nicest home in the village, much nicer than that woman's house or the plain little place her son Joseph built for his new bride." She paused then and bent to look straight into my eyes. "Well? Do you not think it lovely?"

I nodded my head vigorously. "Oh, I do, Mistress Putnam. I do of a certain."

"Good," said the woman. She released my arm, turned, and beckoned to the girl trailing behind. "Ann, come up here. I want you to take Drucilla's hand. She's come to be your companion, and to help me care for the babies. Hurry now. We are waiting for you."

The strange-looking little girl came to walk beside us. I put out my hand to close over the one she lifted toward me. The hand felt cold, and I wanted to drop it. The child had very pale skin, almost translucent. Looking down at the thin arm, I thought at first that the blue veins were not under the skin at all.

"This is my daughter. Her name is Ann just as mine is and the two of you will be great friends."

Had I been older, I might have seen better what to do, but I was only twelve and full of a motherless child's terrible yearnings. Had I been older, I might have waited until no one watched and then walked away. Looking back, I do think that I knew before we even went inside the house that this woman and her daughter were deeply troubled.

The girl pulled at my hand. "Are you going to die?" she asked.

Startled by the strange question, I stopped walking. "Drucilla will die one day, Ann," said her mother. "You know that all living things die." She put her arm around my shoulder. "My daughter and I have just been among our dead," she said, and she waved her free hand toward the side of the house where I saw several white gravestones. "Our family cemetery," she said and leaned her head in that direction. "More of us rest there than live in our home."

We moved on to the house. Mistress Putnam reached to open the door and held it for us. I tried then to drop the child's hand, but Ann caught my little finger in a tight grip. We stepped together across the threshold and into the warm kitchen. I had never been in a home that had a kitchen separate from the great hall where most families cook, eat, and do the majority of their living.

A young woman stood at the hearth, stirring a large pot that hung above the fire. "This is Rose, our hired girl," said Mistress Putnam when she had shut the door behind her. Rose looked up from the pot and nodded, but she did not smile. A little boy of about three sat on a hooked rug, playing with blocks, and a smaller girl napped in a very big basket beside him.

The kitchen was large and filled with wonderful smells that made me want to linger, but Mistress Putnam waved me forward, Ann still clinging to my finger. "Ann, dear, take Drucilla upstairs and show her where she is to sleep." Her hands flew to her cheeks. "Oh, but we have forgotten to bring in your trunk."

"There is no trunk." I shrugged. "No trunk and nothing to put in one on any account." Then I remembered, "Oh, but I did leave my lute in the carriage."

"Rose will fetch it." Mistress Putnam waved her hand in direction. "Do you play?" I nodded, and she went on talking. "How delightful! We shall have music in the house." She whirled to look at her daughter. "Did you hear that, Ann?"

"Yes, Mother." Her lips smiled, but her eyes did not.

Mistress Putnam drew her breath in sharply. "But your trunk—do you mean to tell me, you have nothing, nothing but this one garment?" She reached out to gather a piece of the dress between her fingers and thumb. Embarrassment made my face grow hot, but surprise made me forget my feelings. I saw tears come from the woman's eyes. "You poor child, I will have clothing made for you at once. Come down after you've seen your chamber, and I will take your measure."

I followed little Ann through the kitchen door into the great hall. It was a magnificent room with a fire blazing in a huge fireplace. On one wall was a painting of Mistress Putnam as a very young woman, probably just after her marriage. There was a large dark table for company dining, two brocaded settees, and a chair with green velvet upholstery. A huge clock stood in one corner. Against one wall was a staircase that Ann clearly meant we should climb. At the foot, I stopped, and ignoring her pull, I looked around trying to take in the beauty. As I stood there, though, I also took in something else. There was a feeling in this great house. At the age of twelve, I could not have explained it, could not have found the words to define the premonition of dread that made gooseflesh on my arms. Still, I knew things were wrong here even among such beauty. I put one free hand into my pocket to touch the bag containing the tiny painting of my mother's face, and I wished for the millionth time that my mother had lived. Ann jerked at my finger. "Are you coming, then?" she asked. What else was I to do? I nodded, and we began to climb.

About halfway up we heard Mistress Putnam shriek. "You lazy lout, why is the bread not baked? I'll box your ears again." I stopped walking. "Mama doesn't like Rose," said Ann, and for the first time she smiled. "Most of our servant girls don't stay long, but Rose has to." There were three rooms at the top of the stairs. Ann indicated a closed door. "The babies sleep there." She pointed at a second door. "That is mother and father's chamber." She opened a third door and led me inside. "This is mine." A bed with velvet curtains about it stood in the center of the room. "Rose sleeps on a pallet in the kitchen because she is but a hired girl." Ann pointed to the bed. "You will sleep there with me because you are a hired sister."

I did not like her tone, but I said nothing. It was a nice room, warmed and lighted by the sun pouring through the casements. There was even a small fireplace with a fire. Still, I wished I might join Rose on a pallet in the kitchen. The room felt cold, as Ann's hand had. She was a strange child whose wide staring eyes made me uncomfortable. There were two windows and one opened westward. I moved to stand in front of it. Ah, there it was, a thin line of smoke. I leaned close, resting my head against the glass.

"What are you looking at?" Ann pressed her thin body against me.

"Nothing."

"You are! You are looking at that smoke, aren't you?" The child folded her arms in front of her and drew away so that she could study my astonished face.

"And what matter is it if I look at a bit of smoke from a distant place?"

"That is evil smoke," said the child, and her voice sounded deep, like a growl.

I laughed, but it was brought on by nerves, not mirth. "What a strange thing to say. How could smoke be evil? 'Tis only what follows from a fire."

"I think I know where that smoke comes from. I think it comes from the house of a wicked woman. My mother will not like it if I tell her you looked at that smoke."

Anger that surprised me rushed up from inside. Who was this strange little girl? She was three years my junior. Why should I let her push me about? I whirled to look into Ann's face. "Your mother is a grown-up lady," I said. "She is far too wise to think smoke can hold evil. Tell her if you please." I shrugged my shoulders. "It is of no matter to me." I turned to leave the room, and I did not look back.

Downstairs Mistress Putnam sat at the kitchen table feeding the baby girl who had been asleep in the basket. The toddler was blond, like young Ann. In truth, I saw that the sisters had the same shape of face, the same pale skin, and the same light blue eyes. On Ann, though, those features were haunting. On the baby they were quite pleasing. She looked up at me with a smile that turned into a bubbling sort of laugh. "Sausage," she said to her mother.

Mistress Putnam handed the baby a sliver of meat. Then she looked up at me. "She is delightful, is she not?" I smiled and nodded. Mistress Putnam pointed toward the bench on the other side of the table. "Sit down and talk with us."

I slipped onto the bench. "What is the baby's name?"

"Elizabeth. It is from the scriptures, you know."

"Yes," I said, eager to show her my knowledge. "Elizabeth was the mother of John the Baptist, cousin to our Lord."

"That's right." Mistress Putnam lowered her face to the top of the baby's head and buried her lips in the fair hair for an instant. "And it was the name of our Virgin Queen. This Elizabeth could be a queen. Is she not a delight to behold? I know I should not take such pride in her beauty, but I do."

I held out a finger, and the baby grabbed it. "She is pretty."

Mistress Putnam looked down at the table. "I had many sorrows before Ann's birth. Three babies were born to me, three baby girls. The first lived but an hour. The next was with us for three hours, and the last lived for a day. We thought perhaps she would survive. We even named her. Esther, that's what we called her, but the name died with her. When little Ann came, we did not name her for a month. Even then, I could take no interest, and Thomas chose to give her my name. Ann is sickly, yet she has made it to her ninth year. We lost three more after Ann, all born dead. Thomas Junior is three and very strong. Still, it was not until this little treasure came that I could feel any happiness at all."

I felt warm with pleasure, partly because Mistress Putnam's smile was infectious, but there was more. No grown-up had ever talked to me as if I, too, were an adult. Before the smile on my own face could fully form, though, I looked up to see young Ann. She had come quietly down and crept into the room unnoticed. She stood now near the door. I had not liked the child, had been uncomfortable in her presence, but now I felt unbearably sorry for the pale waif of a girl, who had heard her mother speak of her in such a way.

Ann, aware that I had seen her, squared her shoulders and marched to position herself next to her mother. She shot an angry look at me. "Mother," she said loudly, "Drucilla was staring out the window. She was looking for the smoke from that woman's fire. I told her that the smoke came from an evil house. I told her you would not have her spend her time gazing at evil smoke."

Mistress Putnam did not turn even to glance in her daughter's direction. "Ann, that is nonsense. Smoke is not evil." She reached across the table to pat my hand. "Is there a reason for your interest in smoke from Mary Putnam's house?"

"My friend Gabriel. He lives in that house." I paused for a moment, unsure how much I should say, but the woman's face still looked encouraging. "We have been together since the hour of our births. When Joseph Putnam came for Gabe, he told me to look westward at the smoke from his mother's house." I shrugged my shoulders. "It made me feel closer to Gabe to see that smoke."

"You poor thing," said Mistress Putnam, and she lifted her hand from mine to touch my cheek. "Perhaps we should invite this Gabriel to visit."

Ann pulled at her mother's arm. "You said they were evil." She whimpered. "You said that bad woman and her son took what should have been Father's."

"Hush, Ann, you are but a child and cannot understand grown-up matters." She took the baby from her lap and stood her on unsteady legs. "Mind Elizabeth while I talk to Drucilla."

"Drucilla is not a grown-up," said Ann, half under her breath, but she took the baby's hand and helped her walk to the corner of the room where Thomas played with a kitten.

Afraid she might change her mind, I asked, "When? When can we invite Gabe for a visit?"

"I'll send Rose with a note on the morrow. Does he read?"

"Oh, yes, we were both taught our letters, and Gabe was ever so quick with learning. When will you ask him to come?"

Mistress Putnam pursed her lips. "We will make it an open invitation. No doubt Mary Putnam will work the lad hard. He will not find her home a warm and loving one as you find here. We will tell him that if ever he has a free hour or two, he should walk over to see you."

I felt my face twist with worry. "I hope Gabe is not unhappy. Joseph Putnam seemed kind when he came to fetch him for his mother."

"My, dear," said Mistress Putnam, "believe me, I know a good deal more about my husband's half brother and his mother than you could ever know. Evil people are good at concealing their ways, especially on short visits. No, your friend will be worked until his hands bleed. If only I could have known Mary Putnam might ask for the boy." She shook her head sadly. "I could have given him a good Christian home here. I am not even sure Mary

Putnam will take him to meeting. She claims to attend church in Salem Town where she lived before she married Thomas's poor unsuspecting father. Thinks herself too fine for a simple church such as we have in Salem Village, she does, but in truth, I wonder how often she makes the journey." A sad darkness came across her beautiful face, and she sat staring at the table. I sat quietly as well, full of turmoil. Was Gabe truly in such dire circumstances? Suddenly Mistress Putnam gave herself a shake. "Let us speak no more of cruel people." She stood and put out a hand to me. "Come, we must take your measure for Goody Silbey. I've already sent her word that she is to make you three dresses. What colors do you want?"

After the evening meal, I volunteered to take the two young ones upstairs as I understood that to be my job. Mistress Putnam declined my offer. "I may ask you to do that later, at least for Thomas, but I do enjoy rocking the baby myself. You might help dear Rose with the cleanup. She looks tired tonight." She left with the children and Ann followed. Thomas Sr. went out for the evening chores.

Rose looked over her shoulder. "Don't she just beat anything ye ever saw? 'Poor Rose looks tired tonight.'" She imitated Mistress Putnam's voice. "Right she be. Poor Rose is tired of being slapped about the head." She pointed her finger at me. "Don't ye be taken in by her games. That one bears watching, she does."

I wiped at a wet trencher with a drying cloth. "You don't like her, do you?" I asked.

Rose laughed loudly. "I should say not! Ye may find ye self feeling the same after a bit. Oh, sure, she seems to have taken to ye, for the moment." She shrugged. "Mayhap she won't turn on ye. Ye do be that comely, and she does like pretty things. 'Tis why she loves the baby. Still, she could turn on ye at any time. Turn like a top, she does, and ye never knowing why."

"So for what reason do you stay here?" I reached for another wooden plate to dry.

Rose looked over her shoulder again. "I stay because I'm bound. She paid for our passage over here, Mum and me. Mum died, but I've four more long years to work." She sighed deeply. "Before me there was a new girl in this kitchen near about on the week." She lowered her voice. "At times, though, I tell ye, I've considered just walking off. Mayhap I'd as soon go to prison for the debt or take my chances with the weather and the wild creatures as sleep much longer in this house of doom."

"House of doom? What does that mean?"

Rose shook her head. "Ye will know what I mean. Mark my words! Ye will know."

Even standing so near the hearth, I felt a shiver pass through my body. I glanced over my shoulder and saw Mistress Putnam coming in from the great hall. The woman seemed to sparkle, and she smiled warmly when she caught my eye. She was about to have three new dresses made for me, who could never remember having had even one new dress before, only ones outgrown by some other girl. She had promised to invite Gabe for a visit. I wanted to trust her, had to trust her. I turned my head back to study Rose. The hired girl was quite a lot older than myself, mayhap sixteen or seventeen. Her eyes were dull and her plain face wore a sluggish expression. She was not, I decided, very intelligent, and perhaps she was lazy, just as Mistress Putnam had said.

Of course, I had no memory of my own mother. What I would have given to have recollected even so much as a moment with the woman whose tiny portrait was in my pocket. If I closed my eyes and tried very hard, I could remember bits about Gabe's mother, Mary Matson. Mary had been my mother, too, for four years, four years of tender hugs and good-night kisses. I think perhaps it would have been better for that forlorn child I was at twelve if I had never been loved by a mother, but I could remember being held by Mary, could remember her golden hair. Was it because Mistress Putnam had hair of the same color that I felt so drawn to her? Perhaps, but even now, three years later, I cannot explain the power the woman had over me from the first. I can say only that in that kitchen with Rose on the very first evening, I made up my mind to trust Mistress Putnam, more than trust. I made up my mind to love her. I would, I determined, love her unless something big forced a change of mind.

When it was time to go to bed, I dreaded being alone with Ann. She surprised me, though, by giving me a real smile as she closed the chamber door. "You need to know something," she said, and her voice sounded almost friendly. "My mother brought you here for me. She thinks I need a friend."

"Well," I said, trying to keep my voice light, "I shall do my best to be your friend."

Her smile twisted into a grimace and she shrugged. "I don't want you for a friend, but it doesn't matter. You won't be here long."

I had climbed into the bed, and I turned away from her saying nothing. She was not finished with talking. "My mother can see the graves from her window, all my dead sisters and a brother, too."

On the other side of the bed, I pulled the blanket closer. I did not want to talk about dead babies. Ann, though, was determined. "On the morrow you can go there with Mother and me. We visit each day and talk of them. Mother told me she looks out at them just before she goes to bed. It keeps her busy. She does not have time to come bid me good night, but she may come now. She wants you to be happy here."

In the moonlight that came through the window, I could see the outline of the doorway. Would Mistress Putnam come through the door? I knew I should hope that the woman did not come. If she came, Ann was likely to resent me even more. Still, would it not be nice to have her bid me good night?

The door did open. "I've come to say sweet dreams, girls," said the woman, and she walked to stand on my side of the bed. "I hope you are comfortable here, Dru." She bent to brush her lips against my forehead.

"I am very surely comfortable, thank you," I said, and I put up my hand to touch the spot where I had been kissed.

"Good night, Ann." Her mother moved to kiss the younger girl.

"Did I not tell you?" said the voice beside me when the door had closed behind the woman. Ann sighed deeply. "Well, Mother brought you here for me, but she seems to like you more than I do. It is of no matter. I am her real daughter. In the end that will count."

I did not sleep at once. When her breathing left me certain that Ann was asleep, I slipped quietly from the bed and moved to the window. The moon was big and round in the sky, but still I could not see the smoke. I knew, though, where to look. "Gabe," I whispered. "Gabe, can you hear me?" Was he truly going to be mistreated? I thought not. Joseph Putnam had been very pleasant when he came for Gabe. Mistress Putnam was mistaken. Something had made her misunderstand. Already I was making excuses for the woman.

For a long time, I stayed by the window, but then I heard steps in the hall. What if Mistress Putnam should come back to open the door to our sleeping chamber? If she saw me at the window, she might think me unhappy or, even worse, ungrateful. Quickly I slipped back into bed.

The door did open, and the woman came in. "Are you sleeping, Dru?" she whispered.

"Not yet, Mistress."

She moved to stand beside me. "Don't call me Mistress. In

truth, I've been thinking that mayhap you should like to call me Mother. It surprises me how happy I am to have you in the house. I feel close to you already."

I pulled my breath in sharply, but I said nothing. No words would come to my lips, only wonder to my heart.

"What do you think, child? Would it please you to address me so?" Mistress Putnam leaned over the bed.

I could see her bright eyes in the light from the window. "Yes," I whispered. "It would please me much."

"Good! When you are ready, then." Mistress Putnam brushed back the hair that had fallen across one of my eyes. A strange sensation spread through my body. Tomorrow I would get up in this house. Tomorrow I would eat my morning meal at the large table in the kitchen. I would help clean the kitchen, and might well help prepare food for other meals. I would mind the baby Elizabeth and see to Thomas Jr. Yes, I would even be nice to the strange little Ann and try to make the girl smile. Tomorrow I would see the woman, the beautiful, smiling woman. Tomorrow I would call that woman Mother. I whispered the word aloud, "Mother," and then I fell into a deep, sweet sleep in the warmest most comfortable bed ever.

Chapter Three

I woke suddenly in the night and sat up straight in bed. What? What sound was that? I pushed back the bed curtain. Then I knew. Someone was running down the stairs, someone big, whose feet fell heavily on the stairs. Thomas Putnam! He was the only person in the house large enough to make so loud a thud on the steps. I heard the back door being flung open. "Ann," a man's voice called. "Ann, stop! What are you doing?"

I grabbed a blanket from the bed, wrapped it around myself, and ran down the stairs and into the kitchen. Through the open door I could see them. Mistress Putnam stood on a small hill a few feet from the house. She wore a long white nightgown, and she stood near white gravestones, her hands wrapped around the handle of a huge knife, the kind used to butcher hogs. Her arms were bent at the elbows, and the great blade of the knife was pointed at her chest.

"Come no closer, Thomas," Mistress Putnam called. "Come no closer, or I'll plunge the blade into my broken heart."

"Ann, no, let me have the knife, please."

"Leave me be, Thomas. I want to die. I want to die here with my babies."

"You've other babies," her husband pleaded. "What of the

babe you carry? What of young Ann, and little Thomas? What of Elizabeth? You love Elizabeth so. They need you. Think of our living children, woman. Surely, you would not take their mother from them!"

"Nay!" she screamed. "They will be better off without me! The dead babies call to me."

Still standing at the open doorway, I felt as if I might faint. I reached out to hold on to the wall. Do something to help. I must do something, but what? What could I do? Suddenly, I felt a hand on my arm, and I jumped with fright.

"I should have let her do herself in," said Rose. "Heard her, I did, when she come into the kitchen for the knife. I stayed still until she was outside, else she'd likely have drove the blade through me. When it was safe to move, I run up to fetch him. Saved her life, I reckon, unless, of course, she still does the plunge."

I pulled away. I would not stand there with the girl doing nothing. I ran out the door. The earth was cold beneath my bare feet and rocks cut at my skin. I did not slow my pace.

"Go back to the house," Thomas said to me when I was beside him. "Be with the young ones, should they wake."

"No," I said, surprised at the strength of my voice. Turning from the man, I moved slowly toward the woman. "Mother," I called. "Mother, look at me. I'm your Drucilla, and I need you. Please, I have no memory of a mother. Please don't leave me now."

"Drucilla," said the woman. "Drucilla, I forgot all about you." She lowered the knife, and I held out my hand. She grabbed at it as if it were a rope and she was drowning.

"I'm cold," I said. "Can't we go inside?" She dropped the knife.

Just as we crossed the threshold, Thomas stepped from behind us to pry his wife's fingers from around mine. "Drucilla needs sleep," he said gruffly. I thought him brutish and lacking in sympathy toward her. I followed them mutely up the stairs, where he led her to their chamber. I was at the top of the stairs when he turned toward me for a moment. "Thank you," he said. "God Almighty has sent you to her."

I felt better toward Thomas Putnam. I realized then that I was shaking, whether from cold or fear, I was uncertain. I went back to my bed for warmth. What a strange sight I had just seen. Looking back at my twelve-year-old self quaking there under the covers, I long to reach out to her, to warn her, but it is, of course, too late, three years too late.

With the first light, I woke, dressed, and made my way downstairs, leaving Ann still asleep. With each step I wondered what awaited me. From the kitchen came smells of porridge, and I knew that Rose must be at the stove. Would Mistress Putnam remain in bed? Would she send for me to sit beside her so that we could discuss the frightening night before?

Rose was not in the kitchen. Mistress Putnam stood at the stove. She turned and smiled widely, her eyes dancing with joy. "Drucilla, come let us break fast together. Thomas has had his fill and is now at his work. Let us enjoy this time before the young ones wake."

I felt myself shake slightly. Was this the same woman who had tried to end her life just a few hours before? "Where is Rose?" I asked.

"Gone to her aunt's." She tossed her head. "I gave her the morning free. I cannot explain why I am so kind to that creature." She sighed with disgust. "Full of a wild story about last night, she was. I spoke plain to her. 'Rose,' I said. 'Do not carry that foolish story to the village. Should you do that, I would be forced to punish you severely.' That's what I told her."

"She told me she is bound to you." I could think of nothing more to say. I moved into the room.

Mistress Putnam sighed again. "Yes, we paid for her passage, hers and her mother's, God rest her soul. Her aunt arranged it. She owes us four more years. I don't know that I can abide her that long, but I try because it was a large sum we spent."

My mind had raced while she spoke. Did she have no memory of the night before? She was busy now filling a wooden bowl with porridge, and she handed it to me. There seemed nothing to do save ask, "But Mistress Putnam, about last night? You must remember."

She spun around to put her arm about my shoulder. "Oh, yes, my dear," she said. "I remember last night well. I asked you to call me 'Mother,' and you said you would. Yet, here you are this morning calling me 'Mistress Putnam.' You wound me, dear. You really do."

I swallowed back a protest. Surely the woman had not forgotten the horrible events of the night before, but plainly, she did not want to talk about what had happened. I had no wish to make her unhappy. I loved the feeling of Ann Putnam's arm around my shoulder. Mothers put their arms around their daughters. I knew they did. Very well, we would not talk about the terrible night. If I blinked, I would see the image of Mistress Putnam, white gown blowing in the wind, white gravestones, the long blade of that knife in the moonlight. Well, I wouldn't blink! I would play the forgetting game and enjoy a mother's arm around my shoulder.

"You must eat while your porridge is hot." Mistress Putnam led me to the table and indicated where I should sit.

While she filled a bowl for herself, I studied the hem of the tablecloth. She brought her porridge, sat across from me, and poured us each a cup of tea. I struggled with trying to think of something to say. Then a thought came to me. "Will Rose be back later?"

Mistress Putnam looked over the cup from which she drank. "Yes, just before the noontide meal. Why do you ask, dear?"

"Because . . ." I tried not to make my voice sound pleading. "You know, because of the invitation."

"The invitation?" Mistress Putnam raised her eyebrows, questioning.

So she had forgotten about Gabe, too. This one I would push. "My friend. You said Rose could take an invitation to him at . . . you know, the other Putnams'."

Mistress's hands flew to either side of her cheeks. "At Mary Putnam's?" She sighed. "Oh, yes, I remember now. She took in the boy when we took you." She leaned across the table to be nearer my face. "Tell me, dear, how long have you been with us now?"

"Just one night, Mis . . . Mother."

A troubled look crossed the woman's face. "Really? Are you certain? It seems much longer."

I bit at my lip. "Oh, yes, indeed. You are right. I forget how long it has been."

She smiled sweetly. "And you want to see this boy, the one at Mary's?"

I nodded vigorously. "I do. We grew up together, Gabe and I. We were always together."

Mistress Putnam stood, her food untouched, and brushed her hands together. "Well, then, most certainly we shall send Rose to the woman's house with an invitation to visit you." She shrugged her shoulders. "No, we shall do better than that. Would you like to go with Rose? Perhaps we should just send you along. Mary Putnam is a hateful creature, but should we not show her that we are above her evil ways?" She nodded vigorously. "Yes, we will turn the other cheek, so to speak. Show the vicious woman how to behave. You shall go immediately after noontide, but you must promise me you will eat nothing. There are poisons aplenty in that house! Of that I am certain!"

I doubted what Mistress Putnam said about the poison, but even had I believed it, nothing could have kept me from making that trip. Rose, when she had returned, smiled broadly when I told her she and I were to go to Mary Putnam's after we ate.

She was not, however, the best travel guide. Saying nothing, she tromped through the first field, totally ignoring me. I kept my head down to look for holes and struggled to keep up with her. Finally, I could stand the silence no longer. "Are you certain of the way?" I asked just to start a conversation.

"Certain? I should hope I am! Don't I come this way this very morning and every other time I've had a chance to visit my aunt? She lives right near to old Goodwife Putnam."

"Very well, but wait, please. I want to get the brambles from the hem of my dress." I bent to remove the stickers.

Rose made a sort of disgusted snorting sound, but she stopped walking. "Brambles bother ye, do they? Best toughen up, I'd say. Don't even notice them my own self."

Still with my head down, I thought it would be a good time to bring up the night before. "Rose," I said, "do you recollect what happened last night with Mistress Putnam?"

"With your mum, don't ye mean? Ain't it so that she wants ye to address her such?" Rose broke into a laugh.

I was irritated. What right did this girl have to laugh about a person choosing to call another person Mother? I straightened to look the laughing girl in the eye. "Yes, she does. Why does that make you laugh?"

Rose waved her hand. "Oh, pay me no mind. I daresay, ye will find out the answer to that question ye self if ye stay many days in that loony bin."

I concentrated on a nearby tree that was beginning to bud and swallowed back a retort. Living as I had in many different homes, I had learned when to keep my mouth shut. It was not wise, I knew, to make unnecessary enemies. "Has she ever done that before?" I asked. "I mean, run out in the night that way or threatened to hurt herself?"

Rose shrugged. "Don't reckon she's run out in the night, not since I've been there anyway. It's for sure she ain't tried to hurt herself none, and I got my doubts she'd ever do herself harm." She shook her head. "Little Ann, now that's a different story."

"You mean little Ann has hurt herself?"

"For gracious sakes no! Are ye daft? I'm talking about what the woman done to that child."

"Look at the sun!" I pointed upward. "Time is getting away from us. We'd best hurry on! How much longer must we walk?"

Rose made a grunting sound. "Just through another field and a wee bit of a forest." She began to walk on ahead, but she turned her head toward me for a moment. "Don't fret ye self none. I won't tell ye no tales ye don't bid me to tell. Ye will see. That's all I'll say. Ye will see." We trudged on in silence.

When we broke out of the little forest, I spotted Gabriel at once. He stood, rope in hand, drawing water from a well at the side of the house. "Gabe!" I shouted. Waving and calling his name, I broke into a run, left Rose behind, and stopped only a slight distance from him. Suddenly I felt shy. I wanted to dash to his side and throw my arms around him as I had done thousands of times in our years together, but instead I waited—embarrassed and looking down. We were not the same anymore. No longer was it the two of us against the world. We lived in different houses.

"Dru!" He swung the bucket free from the well. "I'm glad to see you."

"I'm glad, too, Gabe, ever so glad." I moved closer to him.

"How do you fare?" I leaned to look into his face. "Is she mean to you?"

He shook his head quickly. "No, she seems a gentle woman."

I turned to stare closely at the house. "You'd best take in the water, take no chance at angering her. Mayhap you can slip out later and talk to me more."

He set the bucket down and reached for my hand. "No, you can come with me. I think Goodwife Putnam will be pleased."

I held back slightly, but he pulled me. "Call the other girl, too."

I turned to Rose, who had almost reached us by then. "My friend says I should go inside." I paused to glance once more at the house. "He says you will be welcome, too."

Rose let out a grunt and moved her head to a haughty position. "Don't trouble ye self to say I'm welcome here. I've visited this house aplenty. Didn't I say my aunt lives right near?" She stepped around us, went to the door, and knocked loudly.

The woman who opened the door had gray hair and a small frame. "Why, Rose," she said. "It is a surprise seeing you here." Then she spotted me and stepped out onto the steps. "I see I have more company." She came toward me with her hand held out. "You must be Gabe's Dru. You are welcome here." She took my hand in hers. "Still, I must ask. Does Ann Putnam know you have come?"

I opened my mouth to speak, but Rose did not give me a chance. "She does. Sent us her own self. I come as a guide for the girl." She walked through the open door.

Goodwife Putnam smiled at us. "Rose doesn't wait to be asked," she said. She waved the two of us inside. The great hall was not as large as the one at the other Putnam place, nor were the furnishings as elaborate. There were no settees, only straight-backed chairs and a rocker. The room had a warmth about it, though, that I could not deny.

Another gray-haired woman sat near the fire. She smiled at me. "Rebecca," said Goodwife Putnam, "this is Gabe's friend, Drucilla. She's in the home of Thomas and Ann, but they've agreed she should come to visit Gabe." Mary Putnam turned to me. "This is my friend, Rebecca Nurse. We knew each other way back when we both lived in Salem Town, when my first husband was alive."

I smiled and nodded my hello. Both of the women seemed pleasant, and I wanted to be polite, but what I wanted most was to know how Gabe was being treated. I searched his face for clues. His eyes were bright, giving no indication that things had been hard for him so far. "Gabe," said Goodwife Putnam, "why don't you take Drucilla into the kitchen for a cup of tea? You might want to show her the draught board." She laughed. "I taught Gabe how to play just yesterday, and after noontide today he was able to beat me at a game."

Gabe nodded. "Come on," he said, and he led the way to the kitchen. It was a large, pleasant room with a glowing hearth and good smells. On the table was a board with squares painted on it. Small, round pieces of wood with lines on them sat on some of the squares. "Want to play?" Gabe asked, and he waved at the board.

"First, I want to talk." I settled myself on the bench and Gabe took a seat across the table. "Mistress Ann Putnam says Mary Putnam and her son, Joseph, cheated her husband out of what should have come to him from his father. She says Joseph Putnam got it all."

Gabe shook his head. "Joseph told me about it when he brought me here. The land Thomas Putnam and his wife live on was a gift from his father. Joseph just got his share after his father died."

I looked down at the floor. Had Mistress Putnam lied to me? I didn't want to think about that. I glanced up at Gabe. That day, when we were newly separated, was the first time, the first of many times to come, when I felt torn between Gabe and Mistress Putnam. I could not tell him how strange a woman I lived with, nor could I tell him how drawn I was to her, despite her bizarre behavior. It felt peculiar to hide something from Gabe, but my decision was made.

"Is something wrong, Dru?" he asked. "What's it like for you over there?"

"It is a lovely house. I was brought to be a friend to the daughter, young Ann, but I doubt she even likes me much. She's . . . well, she's an odd girl. Her mother and father seem to be glad I am there, though, and there are two sweet wee ones."

He nodded. "Goody Nurse has a yellow parrot. I am to go to her house on the morrow to see it. Her sailor son brought it to her, and she says he can talk. Won't that be something? And she has some books I can borrow, too."

I felt a pang of jealousy. Gabe had learned to play this game called draughts and he was excited about a yellow bird. I felt somehow I was losing him. I was glad it seemed unlikely that he would be mistreated, but I would have liked him to be a little unhappy, being away from me.

The door opened and Rose appeared. "I come for a spot of tea," she said. "I reckoned ye two wouldn't be wanting privacy, being too young for courting. Give ye a couple of years, though, and I suspect ye won't want anyone else around ye when ye be together."

Courting with Gabe! What a funny thought! I saw that his face was red. "Rose," I said, "you have daft ideas!"

Rose went to the stove and poured herself some hot water from the teakettle. "Daft? Ye think so now, but mark my words. Ye will be singing a different tune afore we know it."

On the way home, I decided to question Rose. I strained to

keep up with her steps. "Do you know where Thomas Putnam got his land?" I asked.

"I suppose I would know. Everybody does. He got it from his father, the first Thomas Putnam, him what was the husband of Mary Putnam and the father of Joseph."

"Did he buy the land from his father?"

"Buy it? Of course he did not buy it. Neither did his brother, Richard. That's why the magistrate never paid no heed when Thomas and Richard put up the complaint about how Joseph got all that was left of his father's land in the will, even if it was some more than the others got."

"But Mistress Putnam said—"

Rose cut me off. "Folks say I'm dull, but it seems to me ye cannot be oversmart ye own self. Ann Putnam is a bitter, jealous woman, and she's made her husband half crazy, too, them always looking at what Mary and Joseph got and wishing for it. Ye think the woman is pretty and sweet." She made a disgusted grunting sound. "Ye will learn. Even ye has to have that much smarts."

I swallowed hard and let my feet slow to fall behind Rose. I wanted no other conversation. Rose did not like Mistress Putnam, but what was that to me? The woman was odd, I couldn't deny that, but what difference did that make? Mistress Putnam had had her share of heartache, hadn't she? All those dead babies might make anyone strange. I would not listen to what other people said about this beautiful woman who had asked me to call her Mother. That, I knew, was the important thing—having a mother. I could overlook a great deal of perplexing events in exchange for having a mother, couldn't I?" I held my head high. I would simply not listen when others criticized Ann Putnam, and I would tell no one about the strange goings on in the Putnam house, not even Gabe.

Chapter Four

Little Ann saw us from the window and came outside to meet us. "You came back!" She scowled. "Mother said you might not, but here you are."

"Why would I not come back?" I asked.

"Mother did not say why." She twisted her face. "I think she believed Mary Putnam might kill you. Did she say hateful things to you?" She sounded hopeful.

"No." I shook my head. "Goodwife Putnam treated me well."

"But she is evil, though. Mama says so."

I looked at Rose. "I ain't planning no speech on the subject." Rose shrugged her shoulders. "Not wanting my ears boxed, I plan to keep mum."

Inside the house, we found Mistress Putnam in the kitchen, making a meat pie. She wiped the flour from her hands and reached to hug me. "Did you see him, then?" she asked.

"I did, and I like knowing he is but a walk away." My heart beat fast, dreading other questions.

"And that woman? You saw her, too?"

I drew in a long breath. "Yes, she is frightening. I felt . . . glad to escape that dreadful household." I thought then not to close the door on further visits. "Still, I'd gladly face it, to . . . you know, see Gabe."

Mistress Putnam hugged me close. "You are a brave and devoted friend to the boy. He shall need friends badly, living there." She shrugged. "Mayhap a way will be made plain to us, a way to get him out of the woman's clutches."

I looked over Mistress Putnam's shoulder. Rose stared at me, then turned away to stoke the fire. I would agree with the woman now, but gradually I would help her see the truth. I remembered how Thomas had said that God sent me to her. Yes, I would help her. I wanted to change the subject. "There was another lady there, Goody Nurse. Gabe says she has a bird that can talk."

Mistress Putnam released her hold on me and went back to her pie-making. "I trust not the Nurse family. They opposed my sister's husband, Reverend Baylee, who moved here to be the minister in Salem Village before I was wed. That's how I came to be here. I moved with them to help my poor sister. She lost child after child just as I did, but she finally died herself." She made a bitter face. "No I'd not have Rebecca Nurse in my home, and you should warn your friend about her."

I nodded. "I will," I lied, "when next I visit." Rose turned from the stove to shoot me a disgusted look, but I ignored her. "Should I slice this cheese?" I asked Mistress Putnam.

"Yes, dear, you are such a blessing to our household." She reached out to lay a hand on my arm. "Only it troubles me that I have heard you call me by the proper name but once. Mayhap you should ask about the cheese again."

I smiled. "Should I slice this cheese, Mother?"

"That's better." Mistress Putnam began to hum a tune. Then she stopped suddenly and pointed through the open kitchen door into the family's great hall. Through the front window a figure of a man could be seen walking down the road. "Look, the minister is passing by." Her eyes narrowed. "Oh, he thinks he has an excellent situation here, a fine parsonage with a good salary." She laughed, but there was no mirth in the sound, only derision. "See how nimble he is? Well, he may not be so energetic when real trouble hits him." She nodded her head slowly. "Oh, yes, that is about to happen, but he knows it not. I can arrange it now, just as the others made it happen to my dear sister's husband. The strain killed her." She moved then into the great hall, opened the front door, and called out, "Greetings, Reverend, the Lord has given us a splendid day, has he not?"

Standing near the kitchen door, I could hear the minister's voice, but I could not understand the words. I felt shaken. I had attended meeting regularly while living with Jacob Crown's family, but had stood at the back of the building with the other girls as was the custom. In fact, I had stood often with one of the minister's daughters, Peggy, who was about my age. The minister had seemed a nice man. His hair and skin were of a darker shade than most people I had known. He was small in stature, but his muscles were visible even under his clothing.

Gabe had told me that some boys claimed they had seen Reverend Burroughs holding a barrel of molasses over his head with one hand. What was Mistress Putnam planning to do to the Burroughs family? Should I try to find out and warn Peggy?

Mistress Putnam closed the door and motioned for me to come to the front window. We could see the minister going into his home. "'Tis nice having our house just across the road from the parsonage. Gives me opportunity to watch the man and keep track of his evil doings." She turned and looked straight into my face. "Oh, my dear, I see you are disturbed to hear me speak ill of Reverend Burroughs." She sighed. "Of course, you are. It is not easy to hear that a man who claims to do God's work is evil."

"Is he truly?"

"Oh, my dear, he is evil indeed. Do not talk about this to others, but I tell you he is killing his wife!"

"Does she not suffer from consumption? I have seen her be taken by fits of coughing."

"Ah, that is what they say, but I know the truth. He has beaten her, injured her organs." She made a tsk-tsk sound with her tongue. "She'll not last long."

"Can we do nothing to save her?"

Mistress Putnam put up her hands as if to stop me from rushing out the door. "Oh, dear girl, do you not see how dangerous it would be for us to interfere? The man could come into our home while we sleep and murder us all. No, we will remain mum until we can think of a way to turn the church against him."

I could not think how turning the church against him would save his wife, but I did not ask. This was all too much for me. I had thought it might be pleasant living near Peggy Burroughs. I had imagined that the girl and I might become true friends. Gabe had always been my only friend, and I had thought it might be good to have a friend of my own sex. Now I would make no move to know Peggy better. I could not bear the thought of seeing the girl on Sunday, knowing as I did what terrible things were happening in the minister's home. Or were they? How much of anything this woman said could I believe?

The kitchen door was open. I looked into the room to see Rose standing near the hearth. I wanted to spin around, did not want to see Rose's expression. Something, though, would not let me turn, and I looked directly at Rose, catching her eye. She stood silently shaking her head over and over. I stepped to the door, reached out for the knob, and closed it.

"That's right," said Mistress Putnam. "We must not let that simple-minded Rose hear us talk about Reverend Burroughs.

I will lay a plan. God's justice will be done. Don't fret yourself over it, sweet child. Just you let me handle Reverend Burroughs." She moved back then to open the kitchen door. "I must finish the pie for Sabbath dinner."

That night, I was awakened again. This time by crying. I pushed away the heavy curtains that hung around my bed so I could hear better. The sobs seemed to be coming from Mistress and Mister Putnam's chamber. I got up, went to the door, and stepped lightly into the small space at the top of the stairs. Now I could hear voices coming from the room. I moved closer to their door. The faint glow under the doorway told me that a candle had been lit inside the room. Holding my breath, I listened.

"Ann, Ann, you must try not to cry. You will make yourself ill again," Thomas Putnam said.

"Try not to cry?" Mistress Putnam's voice sounded shocked. "Had you seen them as I did, you could not speak so!"

"It was but a dream, wife. Calm yourself."

"No, Thomas, it was more than a dream!" She was shouting now, and the emotion in her voice touched my heart. Why didn't Thomas Putnam try to comfort his wife instead of telling her to calm herself? "I could see them, I tell you," she said. "See them as clearly as I see you now. They were dressed only in winding white sheets, and they stood in a line. My dear sister, her four dead babies, and our babies. Our babies, too, were there, Thomas. How it broke my heart to see their pale, dead faces! They held out their arms to me, all of them, and they moaned. At first they said nothing, only moaned from great pain. Then the words came: 'Murdered, we've been murdered.' Oh, Thomas, what am I to do? How can I find a way to bring them justice?" She let out a terrible screeching sound.

"Ann, Ann, please. It was but a dream. You must think now of our living children, and of the babe you carry. Do not make yourself ill over a dream."

Shuddering, I made my way back into the chamber and into the bed I shared with little Ann. I closed the heavy curtains behind me. I did not want to hear more. It was obvious that Thomas Putnam made no effort to comfort his wife. Poor thing, she had endured so much pain, but she was no longer alone. Providence had sent me to the Putnam home. "I will help ease your sorrows, Mistress Putnam," I whispered into the darkness. "No, that is wrong. I will ease your sorrow, Mother. I promise."

The next day was Sunday. Rose, having the day off, had left the evening before after supper and after preparing the porridge for Sunday breakfast. I washed little Thomas and baby Elizabeth. I tried to help Ann with her hair, offering to put it up for her so that it would stay beneath her white cap, but she only frowned at me and turned away. Mistress Putnam warmed the porridge and laid the table.

Thomas Putnam, I learned, did not like to use the carriage on Sunday. "We've got to walk the mile to meeting," Ann told me as we left our bedchamber. Her voice, to my surprise, did not have its usual angry tone. In fact, she smiled. "Papa always puts Thomas up on his shoulders, and he holds my hand all the way. Mama usually carries Elizabeth, but likely you will have to now because Mama isn't so strong these days."

I wondered if the little girl knew her mother was with child, but I did not ask. It was not seemly that children should discuss such things. Mistress Putnam had told me she had two more months before her time. Again I remembered how frightening childbirth was. I could not let myself think of the danger to Mistress Putnam, but I did think of the baby. Mistress Putnam could not endure the death of another child.

"The way I see it," Thomas Putnam said to me while we waited for Mistress Putnam and Ann to come outside, "the creatures deserve a rest, too. I only use the carriage on a Sabbath if the weather be bitter." For the first time, I looked closely at the man's face. His eyes were kind, and I thought perhaps I had been too quick to think him unsympathetic.

The walk to meeting was a pleasant one. Mister Putnam walked ahead with little Thomas and Ann, just as the girl had said. She seemed a different child with her father, chattering about the coming spring and about a robin they saw. I walked beside Mistress Putnam, and I did carry baby Elizabeth. The sun was bright and warm. I was able to keep all thoughts of the minister from my mind.

Inside the church, men and women separated, men to take their seats on the left, women to the right. I gave the baby to Mistress Putnam, but I took Thomas and Ann to the back, where I would stand with the other children. I had hoped to see Gabe, but he was not among the group. Thomas settled on the floor. From his pocket he took a small wooden top and a string. I had noticed him with the toy earlier, patiently trying to learn how to spin it.

Just before the minister entered, Gabe came in the door, pushed through the group, and came to stand beside me. "I was afraid you weren't coming," I said. "Did Goody Putnam not want you to ride with her to Salem Town for meeting?"

He grinned at me. "She said I could attend either service, my choice. I wanted to see you."

I felt my spirit lift. Gabe had not forgotten me even though he liked his new life, but my happiness was short. He shrugged and added, "Besides, I like Reverend Burroughs."

I grimaced. "I do not trust the man," I whispered, leaning close to him. "I think he beats his wife and makes her ill."

"I don't believe it," Gabe whispered. "Where did you hear such a thing? If Ann Putnam told you that, she has a vicious tongue."

I bit at my lip and dared to lie at meeting. "It was not Mistress

Putnam." I glanced away from Gabe's face. "I promised not to repeat the story, and now I am dreadfully sorry that I did so, but I say again, I do not trust Reverend Burroughs."

Just then the minister entered the building and walked to the pulpit, built up on a sort of stage. He wore a black robe over his clothing, and I marveled that I had never before noticed the sinister look about his eyes.

"Before I name my text," the minister said, "I need to speak of my good wife. Many of this congregation have been most kind to inquire about her and to bring food to the parsonage during her illness. You have prayed for her, too, and now I must entreat you to pray even harder." His voice broke, and he stopped to regain his composure. "Her condition has worsened. Even now she lies in bed with a grievous fever. Our eldest child, Peggy, tends to her."

From my place at the back of the church, I could see the faces of some of the women as they turned to one another, their eyes downcast, shaking their heads sorrowfully. I could see that Mistress Putnam exchanged a distressed look with the woman beside her. For the first time it occurred to me to wonder how Mistress Putnam had learned of Reverend Burroughs's evil actions. The minister gave his text and began his sermon, but I made no attempt to think about his words. My mind was full, going back over my three days spent in the Putnam household.

After the first sermon members of the congregation went home to have dinner before returning for more preaching. Mistress Putnam served the meat pie. When the family had eaten, she took another pie from the cupboard, wrapped it in a clean cloth, and announced, "We'll just drop this one across the street to the Burroughs's house on the way to meeting. That poor family, they've suffered so. Reverend Burroughs looked thin and worn this morning." There seemed to be real pity in her voice, and I strained to understand.

In front of the Burroughs' house, Mistress Putnam put her hand on my arm. "Come with me, dear. It might cheer the poor daughter to see you."

Peggy came to the door. Her eyes were red-brimmed from crying. "Mother's most dreadfully bad," she said. "I begged Father to stay with her, but he says he must preach."

"We will stay with you, child," said Mistress Putnam, and she waved her husband and the children on. Afternoon sermons were always two hours long. Mistress Putnam bathed Goody Burroughs's face with cool water and fed her bits of meat pie. She put Peggy and me to work at cleaning the kitchen. "God will forgive work on Sunday when it is done to help the sick," she explained, and she herself scrubbed the floor.

While Peggy and I were alone in the kitchen, she told me that she feared her mother might die. "I cannot imagine our lives without her," she said.

I handed her some wooden bowls to wash. "Is your father kind to you?" I asked.

"Oh, Father is the kindest man on earth, but still . . ." Her voice choked with tears. She wiped her eyes on her sleeve and went back to work.

I wondered if Reverend Burroughs would object when he saw the clean kitchen. I had often heard ministers criticize those who did not keep the Sabbath sacred, but when he came in, he thanked Mistress Putnam for her work. I watched in wonder while she served the minister a dinner of meat pie.

"This is marvelous," he said, and Mistress Putnam beamed.

On the short walk back to the Putnam house, I decided I had to ask. I could no longer bear the confusion I felt. "You were pleasant to the Reverend." I looked closely at the face beside me.

Mistress Putnam smiled. "Of course I was. He is our minister, is he not? We are lucky to have a man such as Reverend Burroughs to fill our pulpit."

I stopped walking. "But I thought you said that the Reverend beat his wife and caused her sickness."

Mistress Putnam stopped, too, and her hands flew to her face. "What a strange idea. Whatever made you come up with such a notion?"

"Did you not tell me that, just yesterday?" I felt tears stinging my eyes.

Suddenly Mistress Putnam began to cry. "Did I? Oh, the memory comes back. I said terrible things." She reached for my hand. "You must think me a vicious, hateful person."

"No, Mother, never. I could never think such of you."

"Sometimes I say things I don't mean." She wiped her eyes with a handkerchief. "I am going to tell you something, Drucilla, that I have never told anyone. I think I may be bewitched!" She drew me closer to her. "That awful Sarah Good, you know, the beggar woman?"

I nodded. "I know her."

"I believe she has cursed me because I refused her food once. She knocked at my door when I was not well, and I yelled at her to go away." She began to tremble. "How I dread her knocks."

Bewitched! Suddenly all that had happened made sense. Witchcraft was a very real danger to us in Salem Village. What could I do for this suffering woman? "I will answer the knock when we know it is Goodwife Good," I told her.

"You are a treasure!" Mistress Putnam dried her tears. "And you will keep my secret, tell no one when I am not rational?"

"I will keep your secret, of a certain, and I will help you always."

"What a fortunate day it was when you came to be my daughter!" She took my hand and we walked on.

Chapter Five

For a time, life was quiet in the household. I thought often of what Mistress Putnam had told me about being bewitched. The poor woman, my heart ached for her, but I must admit, too, that a feeling of importance grew inside me. This grown-up lady had shared her grievous secret with me. I alone understood her.

Goody Silbey made me an entire wardrobe. There were three dresses—a gray linen, a brown one for everyday wear, and a soft blue for special occasions. She also brought a nightgown, petticoats, and aprons. I took up the blue dress and held it to my cheek. "I've never had a new dress before," I said. "Not that I can remember, anyway. They've always been ones someone else outgrew."

"Go put one on and show us how it fits," said Mistress Putnam.

"I feel like a princess," I said when I twirled around for the ladies to see my blue dress.

"And you look like one," said Mistress Putnam. She turned to Goody Silbey.

"Tell me, Mary, have you ever seen a girl prettier than my Drucilla?"

Goody Silbey looked uncomfortable for a moment. "I am not

sure 'tis good to let the girl hear you say that. Pride is a dreadful sin, you know." Then she shrugged. "But, truth be told, she is a most comely girl."

I felt my cheeks flush. I had never been called pretty before. Then I saw young Ann, sitting quietly with her doll near the hearth. The girl looked so sad. After Goody Silbey leaves, I would try again to befriend her. Then I spied a long piece of the blue material lying on the table. Clearly it belonged to Mistress Putnam, else Goody Silbey would have left it at her house. It was enough, I felt certain, to make a girl's dress. I thought I could do the work myself.

I moved over to the table, picked up the cloth, and waited for the conversation between the women to pause long enough for me to speak. "Mother," I said, "I am wondering if you have plans for these goods?"

Mistress Putnam looked up from the tea she poured for Goody Silbey. "Why do you ask, dear?"

"I hoped I might be allowed to make a dress for Ann." I looked over at the younger girl and smiled. "I think I could do it."

"How kind of you!" Mistress Putnam set down the teapot, folded her hands beneath her chin, and beamed at me. "Certainly. Take the cloth and my sewing basket."

"Thank you," I said, and I held out my hand. "Come, Ann, let's go work on a pattern to fit you."

Ann did not take my hand, but she did climb the stairs with me to our chamber.

While I took her measurements she said nothing. The silence felt heavy about me, and I began to hum "Greensleeves" softly. I had started to work on a pattern when she spoke. "It is kind of you to make me a dress." A bit of a smile seemed about to appear, but it didn't materialize.

"I will enjoy doing it," I said.

She shrugged her shoulders. "It won't make any difference, though," she said flatly.

"Difference? Difference in what?" I asked.

"The dress won't make me like you."

I suppose I must have looked shocked or hurt because her voice sounded a bit kinder as she continued to talk. "Don't fret. It is just that I don't generally like people." She tossed her head. "Mama doesn't like people, either. I know she seems to like you now, but that is likely to change."

I stared at her, unbelieving. Her face seemed strangely old, her eyes empty. What was wrong with this child? For a moment Rose's remark about young Ann being hurt by her mother tried to push its way into my mind, but I did not want to think about it. I regained my composure. "I am most sorry to hear that you will never like me," I said, "because I think it likely that I will be here for some time. We would be ever so much more comfortable sharing a chamber and a bed if we could be friends."

The girl said nothing. She looked at me with a clear, direct gaze, then shrugged her thin shoulders, turned away, and left the room.

The strange thing is that I was wrong about our being uncomfortable together. Rather, Ann's comment made our relationship easier. I stopped trying to do things for her, stopped trying to win her over. I did finish the dress, but I made no more efforts to help her with her hair or anything else. We shared our bedchamber in a sort of truce. Mistress Putnam seemed at peace, and I had hopes that our dark days were behind us. Later that same week, I started out alone to see Gabe.

In the barnyard behind the Putnam home, a cow had just given birth to a new calf. Thomas Putnam saw me through the half-open door and called out an invitation to come inside. "She's just new," he said, pointing at the little animal, standing on spindly legs and being licked by its mother. "A new birth—now that's a blessing, when the baby's strong like this one." He frowned. "Terrible hard when the little one comes into the world too weak."

I knew he was thinking of those babies whose white tombstones stood on the nearby hill. For the first time it occurred to me that Thomas Putnam had suffered, too, not just his wife. I wanted to say something to acknowledge his sorrow, but I couldn't think of the right words, so I stayed quiet and he went on talking. "Truth be told, it was my idea to bring you here for little Ann. She's got that cursed streak of melancholia, like her mother." He shook his head. "Seems, though, it's my wife who finds the most comfort in having you, and God knows, I am grateful for anything that eases her pain."

"I'll do my best to help," I said.

"She was different when we were first married, before all her grief. Why, she was always laughing, and beautiful. Of course, that last hasn't changed. I do all I can to make life easier for her." He turned toward the barn door. "Think I'll get little Thomas and Elizabeth. Ann, too. The calf will make Ann smile."

I watched him hurrying toward the house, anxious to share his joy in the newborn animal. I felt glad for the chance to see the baby calf and for the opportunity to understand Thomas Putnam better.

My last trip to see Gabe had been only slightly more than a week earlier, but spring had worked hard since I had traveled that path. The fields had small spots of green here and there as I made my way, paying careful attention to go in the right direction. I stopped to touch a branch of the tree where I had earlier noticed the tiny green buds, much bigger now. New life, I thought. It always comes.

Goodwife Putnam opened the door for me and said that I

should go into the kitchen where I would find Gabe reading. The squeak of the door made him look up from his book. He held it up for me to see. "*The Pilgrim's Progress,*" he said. "I borrowed it from Goody Nurse. It's a great story." His voice was full of excitement. "She is most unusual, a real scholar. I am to study with her, the Bible and her books. I never hoped to have such an opportunity."

"I am glad for you," I said. "I have no news for you except that Thomas Putnam's cow has a new calf."

"I've something else to tell you," he said, and he pointed to the bench across from him. "Come sit down. It's not good news."

Sliding between the bench and the table, I fought the desire to hold my breath. I dreaded his words. "What?" I said when I was settled.

"It's about Reverend Burroughs." He sighed heavily. "He is leaving. The church committee declared they would no longer pay his salary."

"Why?"

"You should ask Ann Putnam!" Gabe frowned and looked directly into my eyes.

"Mistress Putnam? What does she have to do with this?" Gabe's arm rested on the table. I reached for it and held on.

"It is the rumor. You know, about the Reverend beating his wife. Goody Nurse and Goody Putnam say she started it. You know she did, and others were eager to repeat the lie."

I shook my head violently. "She didn't. I don't believe she started it."

Gabe slapped his hand down hard on the table. "It was an evil thing to do," he said.

I put my hands over my eyes and scooted my body away to the end of the bench. "If she started the rumor," I said softly, "she didn't mean to cause trouble."

"That makes no sense. How could she not mean harm by spreading such lies?" His brow was knit in anger.

For a short time, I did not answer. I studied the large iron skillet that hung on the kitchen hearth. I had to tell him. "Sometimes she does things she can't help. I fear she may be bewitched."

Gabe sighed again. "I think her more likely to be the bewitcher than the bewitched. I fear you are under her spell. Goodwife Putnam says her husband is. She says he does whatever she wants him to. The woman insisted he file a lawsuit against Joseph."

"You don't know her," I said. "If you knew her as I do, you would not speak so harshly of her."

"I wish you did not live there," said Gabe.

"I wouldn't leave Mistress Putnam. She needs me."

We tried talking about other things, even tried playing a game of draughts, but neither of us could put our minds to it.

The visit was a short one. I left with a heavy heart. Gabe and I had never argued so seriously before. I remembered Gabe's words "Let the Putnams fight each other. It is no matter. They can't separate us." They were, though.

Back at the Putnam home, I saw a rider leaving the front of the house as I approached the back. I hurried to see the man as he disappeared from sight. I thought I knew who he was. Inside I found the children in the kitchen with Rose.

"Mama's upstairs," young Ann told me when I asked.

"Was that Joseph Putnam I saw riding away?" I asked.

"It was," said Rose without turning from the hearth where she stirred a large kettle. The mistress went upstairs when he left. "None too happy." She shook her head. "None too happy a'tall."

"He yelled at Mama," said Ann. "He made her cry."

I moved quickly to the stairs. About halfway up, I began to

hear sobs. The door to Mistress Putnam's chamber was open, and I could see her lying across her bed. I knocked on the open door, and she sat up, wiping at her eyes with the back of her hands.

"What is it, Mother?" I moved to stand beside the bed. "What makes you cry?"

"Joseph Putnam was here," Mistress Putnam said, sniffing between words. "He said terrible things to me." She hiccuped a sob. "Said I have a wicked tongue. Said I've spread lies about Reverend Burroughs."

A large strand of golden hair had slipped from beneath Mistress Putnam's white cap, and I reached out to tuck it back. I felt somehow like a mother to her. She threw her arms around my waist and buried her face in my brown dress. "I did not," she said into the garment. "I swear I did not."

"There, there," I said softly, as one might speak to a baby. "You must not let his words trouble you."

Mistress Putnam pulled away. "You believe me, don't you, dear? I would never tell you a falsehood."

I bit at my lip. For one instant I hesitated, then I made up my mind. "I believe you, Mother," I said, and I nodded my head as if to emphasize the words to myself.

"Good," said Ann Putnam. "A daughter must believe her mother." Suddenly she laughed. "Who knows, mayhap Reverend Burroughs does beat his wife." She shrugged and her smile was big. "There must be some truth to the story. Where there's smoke there is fire, you know."

Chapter Six

That evening, just after supper, someone knocked at the kitchen door. Rose and I looked at each other. We had been cleaning after the family meal, and Rose stood holding a wooden plate above the pan of water. "I'll see who it is," I said, but I hesitated. "It may be Joseph Putnam back to cause trouble." I moved to look out the window. At the door stood Sarah Good, the beggar woman Mistress Putnam feared. I would get rid of her. I reached for the half loaf of bread left from the meal. The knock came again, and I threw open the door.

"I am hungry, miss," said the woman, "as is my child." She motioned to a small girl who half hid behind her dirty skirt. "Will you help us?"

I held out the loaf. "Take this," I said.

Sarah Good scowled. "Bread only? Can such a fine house give no more than bread?" The woman leaned her head through the door opening and looked about the room. "Where is the mistress? Is she unwell?"

"Mistress Putnam is upstairs putting her children to bed," I said, trying hard not to shake. "Why would you think her unwell?"

Sarah Good laughed, a loud, ugly sound. "She is with child, is she not?"

I did not answer. Instead I turned back to Rose. "Get me that hunk of cheese," I said.

"Well," said Rose, "you take the blame then. She don't usually get that much from this kitchen." She handed the cheese to me, and I shoved it at the woman and slammed the door.

That night it began to rain. Lightning split the dark, lighting the bedchamber where I lay, trying to sleep. The rain pounded heavily against the roof and windows. A great cold came over me, and I pulled my heated brick close to my feet.

The next day the rain still fell, and Mistress Putnam's pains started. Rose had already made the breakfast porridge, and I had laid out the wooden bowls and the spoons used for the morning meal before the mistress came downstairs. She was pale. Her hair had not been freshly put up and pieces of it hung from beneath her cap. Her eyes were clouded, and she moaned softly and held to the table.

Thomas Putnam came in from the barn carrying a bucket of milk just after his wife entered the kitchen. He peered closely at her. "Are you unwell, my dear?"

She shook her head. "No, just tired. I did not rest well last night."

A scowl formed on Thomas's face. He set the milk bucket on a cabinet. "It's that cursed half brother of mine and his ridiculous accusations." I noticed that his fist was clenched. "I should go to his house and beat him until he begs our pardon."

"No, Thomas, please, let it be." Mistress Putnam took her place at the end of the table. No one spoke during the meal.

Mistress Putnam made no motion to move when breakfast was over. After her husband had gone out the back door to his work, she called to her daughter. "Ann, take Thomas and Elizabeth into the great hall, and play with them." She reached out to squeeze young Ann's hand. "Keep them happy, all day. Do you hear me, child? I am counting on you."

Ann nodded her head solemnly. "Yes, Mama," she said, and she took Elizabeth into her own small arms. I moved to get up, so as to take the baby myself, but Mistress Putnam shook her head and held out her hand to stop me.

"No, Drucilla," she said. "I need you to stay with me." She put her finger to her lips signaling that nothing more should be said until the children had left the room.

"What?" I said when the kitchen door had closed behind little Ann. "What is it?"

Mistress Putnam put her hand on her stomach. "The babe," she said softly. "I've had pains for a couple of hours now."

I jumped up, pushing the bench back with my legs. "What? The babe? But it isn't time! I thought you would have almost two months yet before your time?"

Mistress Putnam nodded. "I do." She looked up at Rose, who had begun to stack the wooden bowls. "Take a knife, the big one, Rose, and put it under my bed. Perhaps it might cut the pain. At least that is what the old women of the village used to say when I was a child." She reached her hand out for mine. "Help me back to my bed, daughter. Neither of you is to say anything of the pain to Thomas, should he come back into the house while I am abed. Tell him I have a headache, and have asked not to be disturbed."

Mistress Putnam pushed against the table with one hand and leaned heavily on my arm as she rose from her chair. "Should I run for the midwife?" I asked when at last we had climbed the stairs and Mistress Putnam was on her bed.

"No," she said. "Surely the pain will go away. Surely God will not suffer this child to be born so early. Does He not promise that we will not suffer more than we can bear?" Her mouth tightened in pain, and I felt the cold fear that had begun to grow inside me downstairs break loose to chill my entire body. "Stay with me, Drucilla, and read to me from the Bible." She pointed to the large black book that rested on a table near the bed.

"What should I read, Mother?" I hated how shaky my voice sounded in my own ears as I began, "The Lord is my shepherd . . ."

Before I got to the last line of the Psalm, Mistress Putnam was moaning in pain. "Fetch Thomas," she said between her teeth. "Send Ann for him." She sucked in her breath, and then went on speaking between clenched teeth. "Send Rose for the midwife." I turned at once to the door, but the woman reached out and made grasping motions toward me. "Come back to stay with me as soon as you can."

I raced down the stairs, yelling directions to Rose and little Ann. I looked about the great hall. Baby Elizabeth slept peacefully on a mat near the hearth. I scooped the sleeping child into my arms. "Come up to the nursery with me," I told little Thomas. I would put the baby safely into her crib, and leave the little boy in that room, too. He could amuse himself with his blocks until his sister came in to be with him.

About halfway up the stairs, a scream tore through the air. "What's wrong with Mama?" little Thomas asked, and he stopped walking. My mind raced. What words were there to explain to the boy? Just then, though, I heard the back door slam and the sound of Thomas Putnam's heavy boots could be heard as his running feet struck the wooden floors.

I did not move. Then the man was pushing by me on the stairs. "Take those babies back down, girl," he said. "Ann's there, too. Keep them in the kitchen."

"Father . . . ," the little boy said, but the man did not appear to hear him. In a second, he was up the stairs and entering the bedchamber. I thought about protesting, about yelling after him that I had been instructed to return. I did not protest. Hadn't I rather be downstairs with the children? Wouldn't anything be better than being in that room and watching the terrible pain?

"Come," I said to the little boy. "I will make you hasty pudding, and I will help you with your top."

"But Mama," he protested.

"We must go to the kitchen, just as your father has told us." Holding the baby with one arm, I reached for his hand again and began to go down. "Your mother will be fine after a bit." I glanced back over my shoulder. "I am sure she will be fine."

For what seemed to be a long time, I stayed in the kitchen with the children. Young Ann would not be amused. "Come taste this hasty pudding," I urged her, but Ann did not even glance my way. Instead she stayed in a corner of the kitchen as far from me as she could get. Hunched on a barrel of molasses, she sat with her thin arms wrapped around her small body as if for warmth.

The baby, after she woke, had to be tethered to the table with the strings on her dress made for such times so that I could use my hands to cook.

Finally, I heard the noise of a horse and cart. The midwife! I wiped my hands on my apron and ran to open the door. Rose led the horse through the rain toward the barn. A large woman burst across the threshold. Taking off her dripping black cape, she tossed the garment toward me. "Spread this near the fire," she said. Over her gray dress she wore a full, white apron with big pockets full of scissors, bandages, bottles, and other tools of her trade.

"Where's she at?" she asked, her body already leaning toward the door into the great hall. Before I could answer, the woman swung her bulk around to peer closely into my face. "You're her!" she said. "You're the girl what was born to poor Jayne Overbey.

I've kept my eye on you, I have, over the years. What brings you here?"

"I live here now," I told her, and I stepped around the woman and moved toward the door, leading the way.

The midwife's hand shot out to grab my arm. "Point the way," she said. "I don't want you around my delivery, nowheres near. Rather you not even be in the house. Have you never stopped to think? You'd be bad fortune to a birthing mother, girl!"

I froze, my foot in midair. "Bad luck? Me?"

The woman nodded her massive head. "Of a certain! Your poor mother dying the way she did." She shook her head vigorously. "No place near my work!"

I shrank back for an instant, then opened the door, pointing through the great hall toward the staircase. "Mistress Putnam's up there," I said softly.

"Boil me some water, but mind you not haul it up to me yourself. Send the kitchen girl with a pail." She tromped through the door and into the hall. I let the door swing closed after the woman, but I could hear the sound of her heavy steps on the stairs.

Heart pounding, I turned to my work. I picked up the wooden pail of water from the table and poured it into the great kettle hanging near the fire. Rose came in then from the barn and went to stand before the fire in an effort to dry herself. "When this water's hot," I said, "you'll needs take it upstairs to Goody Curry. She won't have me in the room, says I'm bad luck because my mother died giving birth to me."

Rose turned to dry her backside. She shrugged her shoulders. "Ain't no luck to be had anyway, not with the babe come so early. It won't live."

I shuddered. "It might. Mistress Putnam says mayhap she has counted wrong. Mayhap the babe is not so early as we think." I moved to look into the kettle. "Here, it is about to boil. Soon I'll dip up a pail."

Rose had barely gone up the stairs, when she was back in the kitchen. "She wants ye," she said. "Goody Curry said no, but she started to scream, said it was her baby and she didn't believe ye could bring ill fortune. Screamed until the midwife said I should tell ye to come up."

I hesitated. I did not want the midwife to blame me if the birth did not go well, but what could I do. I looked at the little ones. Elizabeth had fallen asleep again on the floor, and little Thomas looked sleepy, too. "See to the young ones," I said. "Lizzy-beth needs a cover."

Rose made a huffing sound. "I was tending these babes afore you ever set foot in this house," she said.

"I know," I said softly, "and, Rose, say a prayer for Mistress Putnam."

Rose sighed. "I've done that already, too. Don't like the woman much, and that's a fact, but I wish her no harm, nor the babe, neither."

I left the kitchen, walked through the hall, and stopped at the foot of the stairs. I did not want to go up. A scream of pain came from the room above, and then I heard my name, "Drucilla." I drew in a deep breath and began to climb.

Thomas Putnam sat on a wooden stool just outside the door. "They don't want me inside," he said, "but Ann's been calling for you. Go on in, girl, and see can you bring her any comfort. I'm going to the barn to build a box. Call me. . . ."

I did not ask the purpose of the box. "I'm afraid," I said, but Thomas, on his way toward the stairs, did not respond. I pushed to open the door slightly.

"Drucilla, dear," called Mistress Putnam from her bed. I felt shocked to see her. Her face was gaunt and pale. Sweat dripped from her forehead, and her golden hair stuck out on all sides of her head. She held out her hand. "Come, sit beside me, please."

The midwife stood at a dresser, dipping her instruments into the bucket of hot water. I met her gaze. Goody Curry rolled her eyes, then beckoned with her hand. "It's her funeral, hers or her babe's, but I don't have to like it, that's what."

I bit my lip and moved slowly to the bedside, where I took Mistress Putnam's hand, surprised to find it cold. I looked into her glassy eyes. "Is the pain terrible?" I whispered.

"I can bear the pain," she said through gritted teeth, "but I cannot bear to lose this child." I looked up at the midwife's sad face and saw her shake her head. I turned my attention back to Mistress Putnam.

"Let me get a wet cloth to cool your face, Mother." I moved to the washbasin and came back with a damp cloth. At the bedside, I found that Mistress Putnam had closed her eyes, and I looked quickly to see that her body moved up and down as she breathed. "She's only asleep," I whispered. "She won't die, will she?" I whispered to the midwife

Goody Curry sighed deeply. "Not for me to say, girl, but I'd guess not. The babe, though . . ." She did not finish the sentence. "Ann Putnam's had a deal of sorrow, and now one more."

"Should I go?" I looked at the door I had left partially open.

"Oh, likely I was wrong about the bad luck. Don't know as it really matters, you being here, but get yourself a chair. Can't stand no pacing, that's what." I took a straight-backed chair from beside the washstand and moved it alongside the bed. "You are the very picture of ye mother," the woman said when I was settled.

I gasped. I had dared to think I looked like my mother's miniature, but I was afraid it was only wishful thinking. "No one has ever said that," I said. "Not many here about really knew her."

I reached out to finger the bright squares of the quilt that was folded at the end of the bed.

Goody Curry nodded. "She was just new here, but she was a beauty, same as you are." She studied me, her head cocked to one side. "You will be a taller woman, I'd say, than she was, unless ye have already reached your height. She were short, about the size you are now. I remember how her bare feet didn't hang low when your father carried her." She sighed. "I hope she never knew she was dying and leaving you." She smiled. "It's mightily proud she'd be of you." She told me the story then of the two men who had come to her door and of the births that followed.

A lump came up in my throat, and I felt like crying. "Thank you," I murmured. I stared about the room. On the wall was a portrait of a dignified-looking lady in a blue dress. The midwife followed my gaze.

"That is Mr. Thomas's mother," she offered. "She died more than twenty years ago. I'd say their offspring expected their father to follow soon, but the old fellow fooled them. Up and remarried he did and sired another son. Reckon you know about the bad blood between Mr. Thomas and his half brother, Joseph." She shook her head. "Ugly business. Thomas and his brother Richard even took Joseph and his mother to court. There is no denying that the last born was his father's favorite, just like Joseph in the Bible. Something bad is bound to come of brothers hating each other, half or not."

Mistress Putnam, roused by another pain, sat up and screamed, "It's coming, the baby comes!" I rose to leave the room, but Mistress Putnam grabbed at my arm. "Stay with me, please."

The baby girl did not keep us waiting long. I knew that she was born alive because I heard the pitiful cry, like the mewing of a tiny kitten. The midwife cut the cord and wrapped the baby in a soft piece of blanket. The cry did not come again.

The woman laid the baby on the dresser. Her large body blocked the view as she worked over the small form.

"Is she all right?" called Mistress Putnam, but the midwife did not answer. Instead she turned to me.

"Send for the father," she said. When Thomas Putnam stepped inside, the midwife made her announcement. "Breathed just once, she did. Poor little creature, just too small for living."

"Do you want to hold her, Ann, before I take her away?" Thomas Putnam asked. His wife said nothing, only shook her head, lay back on her pillow, and closed her eyes.

"Let her sleep for a while," said the midwife. "I'll sit with her."

Unsure of what I should do, I looked at Thomas Putnam. "Come with me, girl," he said. "Someone should be there when I put her in the ground. Someone should be there to bow a head with me." He picked up the tiny bundle, and I followed him down the long flight of wooden stairs. Our footsteps seemed to echo through the house. "We'll go out the front way," he said to me when we were in the great hall. "Don't want to go through the kitchen and stir up the little ones."

The rain had stopped. The air was still damp, the sunless day gray. I followed Thomas Putnam's silent form through the mud and around to the side of the house. Near the other graves, he stopped. "You hold her," he said, "while I fetch the box and dig the hole."

She was light, not as heavy as a good-sized loaf of bread. The blanket had been laid to cover her completely, but when Thomas was gone, I folded it back to see her face. The tiny features were perfectly formed. "Oh," I whispered. "You were beautiful." I choked back a sob. "Oh, sweet, beautiful little angel, I wish you could have bided with us even for a short time." I touched the white cheek. "Mayhap my mother has greeted you in heaven. Even now she may hold you and sing to you a lullaby."

The earth, soaked with rain, gave way quickly to Thomas Putnam's shovel, too quickly for me. I was not ready to hand the baby to her father, not ready to watch him place the bundle in the box, nail down the lid, and lower it into the grave. When the job was finished, Thomas bowed his head, but no words came out, only a sob. I touched his arm, and he looked up at me. "Can you pray, girl?" he asked brokenly.

I closed my eyes and began, "Our father, who art in heaven . . ."

For two months, Mistress Putnam did not speak a word, and she seemed to recognize no one. She ate no meals, only scant mouthfuls here and there. I made the herbal tea prescribed by the midwife and sat beside her as she sipped it. Nothing seemed to help. Thomas journeyed to Salem Town, to bring a doctor who checked her over. " 'Tis no ailment of the body," I heard him say from where I had stationed myself outside the only partially closed door. "The woman's spirit is broken." He made a tsking sound with his tongue. "Perhaps with time, I really cannot predict."

I spent my days tending to the little Thomas and Elizabeth. I grew very fond of the children. Elizabeth was learning to talk quite well. Often I would sing to them and play songs on my lute. Ann continued only to tolerate me. Nothing eased her sorrow, and she spent hours standing quietly in the corner of her mother's room. Refusing to sit, she stood hunched, leaning against the wall and remaining as silent as her mother.

Something of a bond had grown between Thomas Putnam and me. "I've put the babe's stone in place," he said to me one evening as I took the little ones upstairs for bed.

"That's good," I said to him, and the sadness of his face broke my heart. I knew he thought his wife had gone from him forever.

That night after Ann slept, I rose, went downstairs to a window, and stared out at the cemetery. I did not know where Thomas Putnam got the white stone, but the new grave was marked now just as the others were. "You are bad fortune to a birthing mother." The midwife's words ran over and over through my mind.

One morning at the end of the second month, I took Mistress Putnam's tray in to her as usual. She sat up in bed. "Drucilla, dear," she said, "how kind of you to bring me food. I have a mighty appetite." She ate the bread, butter, and porridge that had on other mornings not even been tasted. When the meal was over, she threw back the covers. "I've got to get up," she said. "I know I've been abed a long time, but I cannot think why." She looked closely at me when I went to take her arm.

"You must lean on me, Mother," I said. "You will be weak after so long an illness."

"But, Drucilla, you must tell me about the illness. Why have I been so long in my bed?"

I looked away from her toward the window from which the graves could be seen. I had to tell her. She had a right to know. I drew in a deep breath. "You had a child, a baby girl," I said softly. "She came too early and lived only a moment. You've been... unwell since she was born these two months ago."

Mistress Putnam dropped back to sit on the edge of the bed. "A baby," she repeated slowly. "I had a baby girl who lived only a moment." She closed her eyes. "I did not hold her, did I?"

"No, you said you would rather not."

"I wish I had held her. Did Thomas bury her beside the others?"

"Yes, he did."

Mistress Putnam opened her eyes and looked up at me. "I remember now," she said. "I remember my baby, and I know why she died."

Would she say that the baby died because I had brought bad fortune? I wanted to back out of the room. "I told you. The baby came too soon," I said softly.

Mistress Putnam pressed her lips together firmly, then spoke, her words as hard as stone. "My baby came too early because I was cursed. Those who hate me—my cruel enemies have cursed me." She was silent for a moment, then added, "They caused my baby to die, but I will get even. My baby was murdered, just as the others before her! My enemies will pay." She held out a hand to me. "Come help me to walk to the window so that I can look out and see where she rests."

I went to her. Mistress Putnam put an arm over my shoulder so that she could lean on me while walking. We moved slowly toward the south window, but we stopped in front of an east window to rest. Mistress Putnam lifted her other arm to point. "Look, someone is unloading a wagon in front of the minister's house. I do not know that man or woman."

"He is Deodat Lawson, our new minister and his family. They've only just arrived today."

"A new minister?" Mistress Putnam looked distressed. "What has become of Reverend Burroughs?"

I did not wish to get into a discussion about Reverend Burroughs. I pulled at Mistress Putnam's arm. "I believe he has gone to Maine. Come, you can see the new stone."

Mistress Putnam did not budge from the window. "But why? Why did Reverend Burroughs leave us? He was such a fine man of God."

"I don't know," I muttered. "Mayhap your husband can tell you."

Chapter Seven

I lived three years and some months in the Putnam household, years that changed me from a girl to a young woman. Mistress Putnam, never really strong after the death of her baby, spent most of her time at home, often reading the Bible aloud for hours. She talked frequently of her enemies and of the curse upon her. Witchcraft hung always in the air. Still, she had good days when she laughed, and we could see the beautiful woman she was. On those days there was sunshine in the Putnam home.

Her children yearned for her attention, but I was the primary caregiver for Thomas Jr. and even for Elizabeth, once her mother's darling. I grew to love those two with all my heart. Thomas was a serious child, whom I taught to read and write. He was an apt enough pupil, but when it came to projects with his hands, he was truly gifted. Gabe, who visited me often, gave carving lessons to Thomas, and I still have in my possession a small star he made for me. "It's the north star," he told me when he gave it to me. "It will guide you if ever you are lost." He kissed my cheek then, and tears came to my eyes at the thought of ever being separated from him.

Elizabeth was my joy. Her blue eyes sparkled with fun, and her laugh filled the dark, cold places in the Putnam home. She loved my lute, and I always played and sang songs for her and Thomas after I put them into their beds at night. Elizabeth could have had no clear memory of her mother as she had been when I first came to the house. To Elizabeth, Mother meant a woman who sat with an open Bible, reading aloud, a woman who would sometimes kiss her good night, but who had very little to do with her daily life. It was to me she turned if she hurt herself or felt afraid.

Young Ann changed, too. For one thing, she grew tall, taller than I was, even though I was three years older. I had my growth early, but it seemed I was destined to be short, like my mother. Ann, at twelve, had come out of her shell. Looking back on the change, I think it was because a silent mother was better for Ann than the volatile mother she had grown up with. She always looked forward to attending church because it gave her some time with other girls. I saw her smile with them, but at home she was still often belligerent with me and I paid her little heed.

Mistress Putnam did not dote on me as she had before, nor did she have fits of temper. Rather, she was so often silent that when she expressed any interest at all in what went on about the house we were all surprised.

Thomas Putnam was most kind to his wife, frequently urging her to go with him when he drove to Salem Town on business or for supplies unavailable in the village. Usually, she declined without words, just a slight shake of her head. On the rare occasion when she agreed, Thomas's smile lit the room. "She's coming out of it," he said to me one morning when he brought the milk into the kitchen where I worked alone. "Yesterday we had a regular conversation about the church meeting I attended. She's interested in the new minister. That's a good sign, wouldn't you say?"

I did agree with him, and I repeated his words later to Rose. "Don't be thinking ye will find me hoping she comes out of whatsome ever has kept her quiet." She touched the side of her head.

"Why, it's been near two years, I'd say, since I had my ears boxed."

Gabe came often to visit me, just as I went often to see him. I cannot mark the day our relationship began to change, but at some point during those three years it did. By our fourteenth birthday, we were aware of the difference between us, aware that he was male and I female. There was no open talk of courting, but both of us knew. We touched each other less often, and when a touch was necessary it all but brought a spark.

All three of the Putnam children liked Gabe immensely. Often while he and young Thomas carved, Elizabeth would sit at my feet playing with the little animals Gabe made for her, and I would play my lute and sing. Sometimes they would join in. I remember one evening when the sense of romantic feeling between Gabe and me was fairly new. It was a time when I sang "The Water Is Wide" alone.

The water is wide, I cannot cross o'er.
But neither have I wings to fly.
Give me a boat, that will carry two,
And both shall row, my love and I.

I sang the words while looking down at little Elizabeth, but at the last line I looked up at Gabe. His eyes were full of tenderness, too much for me to handle at the moment. I felt my face turn red, and I swallowed hard when I had sung the last word.

Even the young ones could feel something. "Do you love Gabe?" Thomas asked.

I looked down again. "Well, of course I love Gabe." I said. "Are we not told to love one another? And, of course, Gabe and I grew up together as brother and sister."

"Sometimes things change, though." Gabe stood and tousled Thomas's hair. "It's time I said good night."

"Good night," I said, but I kept my gaze down until he left the room. Young Ann stood in the kitchen doorway, and the look she gave me was of pure hatred. I was to remember that look later, remember it well.

Gabe was always polite to young Ann and to Mistress Putnam on the infrequent evenings when she joined the family during one of his visits, but he told me frankly that he disliked them both. "The girl is too much like her mother," he said to me one Sunday afternoon as we walked.

"But the woman has caused no trouble since the business with Reverend Burroughs," I protested.

"Ah," he said, "you've finally admitted what some of us have known all along. She started the ugly rumor about the man."

Exasperated with myself, I sighed. "Can't you feel some sympathy for the poor thing? If you had seen that dead baby, held it as I did, you might understand her heartbreak."

"I wish I could get you away from there. Sure she's been quiet for a while, but I don't believe she will stay that way. The woman is evil. She's made all sorts of trouble for years." We were nearing the Putnam house. Gabe stopped walking and reached for my hand. We were coming home after the second sermon, having gone after the first sermon to the home of Rebecca Nurse and her husband, Francis, for dinner. Rebecca was one of my favorite people, and Gabe loved her deeply. She was, in her seventy-second year, still young in spirit, ready always to laugh at the antics of one of her many grandchildren or of her parrot, Roger.

"I want you to take Roger when I die," Rebecca had told Gabe earlier that day when we sat at her huge table with two of her eight children and various grandchildren. "You know parrots live long lives, and Roger is but young." She laughed. "My family wouldn't treat him right."

"Who could blame us, Mother?" said her son Samuel with a smile. "I swear you like that bird more than you do any of us."

"I love you," said Roger from his spot on Rebecca's shoulder, and everyone laughed.

Now Gabe and I stood on the driveway of the Putnam home. I shook my head. "No, I could never leave the family now. You know how the little ones depend on me so."

"But that woman is crazy and evil!" He took one of Rebecca's apples from his pocket and prepared to bite into it. "You know she is, but you won't admit to that knowing."

I felt my face grow warm. It had been some time since Gabe and I had argued about Mistress Putnam. I could never explain how I felt about the woman I frequently made myself call Mother. I admit that in my mind I always thought of her as Mistress Putnam, but still I loved her, mostly, I think, because I felt the need to protect her from more sorrow. "She spends her days in prayer and Bible reading, searching always for answers. You claim to want to be a minister. I would think you'd find Mistress Putnam's piety to be admired."

"There's a difference between piety and obsession, Dru." Gabe bit into his apple, then held it out to me.

I shook my head to decline the offer. "Actually, I'm glad to say Mistress Putnam has come out of some of her seclusion. She's been taking a real interest in the new minister who might come to finally fill Reverend Lawson's place. I heard her urging Thomas to get others to agree to his terms."

Gabe took another bite of his apple and chewed it before answering. "Leave it to Ann Putnam to come out of her trance for something like that! The Reverend Samuel Parris would not be good for Salem Village! He wants sixty-six pounds a year, an exorbitant salary. He is even demanding to have the church parsonage deeded over to him and his descendants! Have you ever heard of anything so outrageous? He wants thirty cords of wood, delivered and stacked, too. Joseph Putnam, Francis Nurse, and Joseph Porter will never agree to such unreasonable demands."

"Nonetheless, he may well come. There are others in the congregation who want him, and we've had no real minister for a year, only temporary preachers from Salem Town. We are much in need of a spiritual leader."

"We aren't in need of Samuel Parris. He is not a true minister, only wants to be one now that his business ventures have failed."

But Reverend Parris did come to Salem Village. Even though the committee still fought among themselves over his coming and his demands, he came. Now looking back, I can see it was a dark, dark day for Salem Village, that day of his arrival.

PART THREE

Witches

Chapter Eight

They came in the autumn. "Tomorrow's the day," Thomas Putnam had announced during the evening meal the day before. "The new minister and his family are to move in tomorrow." He looked at his wife, and she smiled. I thought Thomas might shout for joy. The dear man was that happy to have his wife interested again in the life around her.

All of us were interested. We watched from an upstairs window—Mistress Putnam, young Ann, and I—as the family moved in. "Look," said Ann with excitement, "he has a daughter who must be very close to my age. Would you not say we are of about the same size?"

"Yes," said Mistress Putnam. "I am told young Abigail there is twelve, just as you are, but she is the Reverend's niece, not his daughter. The younger girl is his daughter, Betty."

"But this Abigail does live with the minister's family, does she not?"

Mistress Putnam did not answer, and Ann put out her hand to touch her mother. "Did you hear me, Mother?"

"What?" said her mother. "What did you say?"

"I want to know if Abigail lives with the minister's family."

"Yes, I am told she does."

Ann put her elbow on the windowsill and leaned her face into her open palm. "Well, then," she said, "Abigail and I will be friends. I have never had a friend before, but now I shall have one right next door."

"The Parris family will be good for all of us," announced Mistress Putnam in a voice more cheerful than I had heard from her in a long time. "Let's go downstairs. I've had Rose bake an apple pie to take to them."

"Oh," said Ann, and she clasped her hands together as if in prayer. "May I go with you to take the minister's family their pie?"

"We will all go, won't we, Drucilla?" Mistress Putnam led the way downstairs. "This is indeed a good day for the Putnam family!"

Once we were across the road, I felt suddenly shy and I held back on the doorstep. It was young Ann who knocked loudly on the door. "I'm your neighbor, Ann Putnam," Mistress Putnam said when the door was opened and we three had been invited to step inside. "This is my daughter Ann, and the young lady still standing in the doorway is my adopted daughter, Drucilla Overbey. We've come to welcome you, and to bring you this." She held out the pie.

The minister's wife reached toward me and with a wave of her hand beckoned me inside. "I am Elizabeth Parris," she said, and she smiled as she took the pie. Her pale face looked tired and thin. I thought that standing next to Mistress Putnam made the woman look even plainer than she would have otherwise looked. She introduced the two girls. Betty Parris looked like a smaller version of her plain mother. Her cousin, Abigail, though, had dancing eyes, dark hair, and a round, full face.

We visitors were ushered into the great hall and directed to seats. Young Ann and I sat on a settee with Abigail. Little Betty settled on the floor beside our feet. "I am twelve, and my mother says you are, too," young Ann said to Abigail when she had a chance to speak.

Abigail laughed. "Oh, won't it be jolly to have a girl my own age to talk to." She lowered her voice so that her aunt, busy talking to Mistress Putnam, would not hear. "Betty is a dear girl, but she is just a baby, really!"

Just then the kitchen door opened, and a brown-skinned woman appeared with cups of tea. She was tall, and she moved with a grace not apparent among the women of our villlage. I loved watching her. She wore a bright shawl around her shoulders.

"This is our slave, Tituba. We brought her with us from Barbados—her husband, too." The minister's wife motioned to the woman. "Set the tea on the table, Tituba." The slave did so, then, bowing, she left the room.

"This is a wonderful day for Salem Village," Mistress Putnam said. "There are many people in our community who need to hear God's word."

"I hope the community will see that Samuel is indeed God's spokesman." A frown played about her lips and distress showed clearly in her eyes. "We only just learned that the church has yet to agree to some of the requests my husband made, requests that we thought had been agreed to."

Mistress Putnam reached out to grasp the hand Elizabeth Parris had stretched toward the teapot. "Don't you fret, my dear. The people of Salem Village will do what is right. My husband and I will see that they do." She let go of the hand and sat nodding her head.

"Really? We are vastly fortunate to have so powerful a neighbor," said the minister's wife. She poured a cup of tea and held it out to Mistress Putnam. I thought the woman's voice held signs of doubt, maybe even sarcasm, but Mistress Putnam did not seem to notice.

"Thank you, dear lady." Mistress Putnam took the tea and had put it to her lips just as the minister came in from the other room. During the introductions, I studied his face. His coloring was dark, his black eyes penetrating. He stood looking down at the group.

I felt uncomfortable under his gaze and glad when he looked away from me toward Mistress Putnam. "So you are our neighbors," he said.

"And your supporters. I have just promised your good wife that she need not worry about the requests you have made of the church." Her smile was bright. "My husband, Thomas Putnam, and I will see to it that all details are adjusted to your satisfaction."

The minister did not smile, only leaned forward to examine Mistress Putnam's face before he spoke. "I think," he said finally, "that you will be a valuable ally in my quest to bring righteousness to this forlorn community."

Betty Parris began to squirm and half rose from the floor. Without looking in her direction her father said, "Betty, do not move about while your father is speaking with a guest." The girl dropped immediately to the floor again. Her back rested partially against my leg, and I could feel Betty's body tremble. The minister spoke again to Mistress Putnam. "Would it be asking too much, dear lady, to suggest that you might send your girls on ahead when you are ready to return home and that you and my wife might join me in my study upstairs? I think you are the perfect person to tell me about the people in my new congregation."

"I should be delighted, sir." Mistress Putnam's eyes danced.

He smiled then. "Very well, I shall take my leave then. Ladies." He bowed slightly and headed for the door.

"A charming man," said Mistress Putnam when he had gone.

The minister's wife smiled slightly. "Poor Samuel, he demands so much of himself and sometimes of others." Her eyes darted quickly toward little Betty.

"A minister's life is not an easy one. I believe I've heard this is his first church. Is that true?"

"Yes, Samuel was in business when we lived on the islands. Coming to this work later than most puts a great deal of pressure on him." She smoothed her dress with her hand.

"It will be my mission to help him." Mistress Putnam smiled and her eyes danced.

I cannot, of course, know what occurred at that meeting, but I believe it was the beginning of the strong and unholy alliance that grew between the minister and his neighbor.

The next day, I had a chance to make a trip to the home of Mary Putnam, where I sat, as usual, at the kitchen table with my friend. "Did you like him?" Gabe asked when I told him about meeting the new minister.

"I would not presume to pass judgment on a man of God." I did not look full into Gabe's face, turning my gaze instead to the pattern in the oak table. "I did notice that his daughter Betty seems to fear him."

Gabe shrugged. "Is this Betty an unruly child?"

"No, she is timid. I did not like to see that she feared her father. Should not a minister be gentle with such a daughter?" As was my practice, I did not tell Gabe that Mistress Putnam had gotten along beautifully with the man. Gabe mistrusted everything that the woman did.

"You said there was another girl, a niece. Did she seem to fear the man also?"

"I saw no such signs." I laughed. "No, I doubt Abigail Williams fears her uncle. She strikes me as the sort of girl who fears no one, mayhap not even God. Little Ann is definitely taken with Abigail. They are of an age. It will please me much if the girl can bring a little happiness into Ann's life."

Gabe tapped his fingers on the table. "Let us hope all we dissenters are wrong," he said. "Mayhap this Parris family will bring happiness to Salem Village." He shook his head slowly. "I'd say we are due a little. There seems, always, to be more gloom in our village than ever there is sunshine." He smiled then. "Let us hope for new sunshine come with the new minister and his family."

Months later, I remembered that comment. I remembered, too, Gabe's dear face and how I had thought that for me the sunshine was to be found in his smile.

Young Ann began at once to be invited by Abigail to pass afternoons in the parsonage. I noticed from the start that the invitations came always after both Reverend Parris and his wife had left the home to visit the sick or do other work required by church responsibilities. I thought only that the girl was not free to pass time with her friend under the watchful eyes of her aunt and uncle. I felt glad to see that young Ann always came back from the visits with a bit of color in her sallow face and a smile upon her lips.

After one such visit in early February, Ann found me upstairs working on lessons with little Thomas and keeping an eye on Elizabeth. I could see the excitement in her face even before she spoke. "Tituba read my palm today." She reached out for both of Elizabeth's hands and began to swing her about the room. "Your sister is to marry a handsome, wealthy young man, Lizzy," she said. "I will buy you ponies, and I will buy Drucilla a fine big house of her very own, perhaps in Boston."

I reached out to take Elizabeth's hands from Ann. "You will

make her dizzy and yourself, too." I motioned toward a wooden rocker. "Sit down and tell me about this fortune-telling."

"Tituba can look at a person's hand and read the future." Ann began to rock the chair rapidly. "She learned in her old home. She says many there have special powers that white people never have."

Just then I became aware that Mistress Putnam stood in the doorway. I wished mightily that Ann had closed the door. Mistress Putnam would, of course, be horrified. Christians were never to dabble in the dark arts practiced by heathens. I feared the woman's wrath would burst out on the girl as it frequently did and that Ann might no longer be allowed to associate with her new friend.

Ann, too, realized her mother's presence, and her hand went at once to cover her mouth. Mistress Putnam swept into the room, her face agitated. Ann kept her eyes down. She stopped rocking and sat perfectly still. I had caught that look on the woman's face, the look of excitement that always came just before an outburst. This outburst, though, surprised Ann and me.

Mistress Putnam took her daughter's arm and pulled her from the rocking chair to stand beside her. "This Tituba, what else can she do besides read your future in your palm?"

Ann hunched her shoulders and stepped as far away from her mother as possible while still being held by the arm. She raised her free arm, ready to shield herself from the expected blows. "I'm sorry, Mama," she whimpered. "I know I sinned by letting Tituba tell me what she saw in my hand."

The woman pulled her daughter close. "No, child," she stroked the girl's hair. "I am not angry. I'm not. I am interested, that's all." She moved to sit in the rocking chair and looked up at us. "Sit down," she said and pointed toward the floor. "We must talk." She leaned to look into the hall. "Thomas, you and Elizabeth should go to the barn to see the new kittens. Close the door after you go out."

When we were alone, Mistress Putnam smiled brightly. "Now, tell me, Ann, do you believe this slave woman really knows things?"

Ann, unaccustomed to her mother's attention, drew herself to sit up straight. "I do believe she knows all manner of things." She reached up to pull at her mother's dress. "You must come with me tomorrow. You can see for yourself. We will wait until the Reverend and his wife go out to visit the sick." She smiled up at her mother.

Mistress Putnam laughed. "Now what would Reverend Parris say should he find me seeking answers from his slave woman?" She shook her head. "No, I cannot go." She pushed herself up from the rocking chair and began to pace the room. In the middle of a turn, she stopped suddenly and whirled to look at me. "You can go with Ann, help her ask the questions."

"What questions, Mother?" Ann asked, and I could hear the excitement in her voice. She liked the idea of doing her mother's bidding. I, however, felt uncomfortable even at the thought.

Mistress Putnam came back to the rocking chair. Settling herself in the seat, she reached to take one of my hands and one of Ann's. "This is our chance to find who took the babies from me," she said, her voice growing strange, almost trancelike. "And our fortune! I seek to know if your father will ever be the most prosperous man in the village as he would have been had not Joseph Putnam cheated him of his rightful inheritance."

"We can go tomorrow. I'll watch for the Reverend and his wife to leave the house." Ann's eyes were shining. "It will be an adventure for us, Drucilla."

I wanted to say no. I wanted to declare I would have no part of the business. Would it have mattered, I wonder now, if I had refused? It is a useless question because I did not refuse. "Yes, an adventure," I said, and I forced a small smile.

That evening when we were in our bed, curtains drawn, Ann surprised me with plans. "We must come to the questions slowly, not just blurt them out. I think Tituba would not like it if she knew Mother had sent us to discover things from her."

"I don't know," I said. "This whole business leaves me uncomfortable. We ought not to be touching the black arts."

"What could be so bad? We will be safe in the minister's house!"

I remembered that conversation later, too, remembered how I lay in the dark afterward, filled with dread.

Ann spent all morning at the window upstairs in her mother and father's chamber. "I can see the whole house from here, and watch both doors at once," she explained. Mistress Putnam gave Ann no chores to do. Rose complained loudly about Ann not helping clean up after breakfast as she usually did, but I left Thomas's lessons to take Ann's place. Occasionally Mistress Putnam would go to the foot of the stairs and call up to make sure Ann still paid attention. The girl even took her noontide meal at the window.

At one in the afternoon, Ann's delighted voice called out, "There they are, both of them! They are leaving now!" Her feet could be heard as she ran downstairs. "Hurry, Drucilla, we don't know how long they will be gone." Ann had carried her cloak and scarf upstairs. She sighed with impatience as I took time to put on my wrap.

With each step through the snow, I wished I could go back to the Putnams' house. Ann hurried in front of me and pounded at the back door of the parsonage. Abigail answered the knock, a broad smile on her face. "I was just going to come for you," she said.

"I watched from the window. Are they to be gone long?"

"Oh, yes." Abigail giggled. "They've gone all the way to Salem Town. Come in."

The parsonage kitchen was not as large as the Putnams', but it was warm and inviting. Betty Parris sat near the big hearth, an open Bible on her lap. "I'm afraid we cannot have visitors today," she said softly. "Father has said that Abigail and I should spend the rest of this day reading scripture."

Her cousin reached out to close her Bible. "Don't be such a simpleton, Betty. How is uncle to know how long we read? Don't you suppose we deserve a bit of fun?"

Betty did not answer, but she did rise and put the Bible on a shelf. Tituba stood at a worktable, cutting pieces of deer meat for a stew. She said nothing, but her dark eyes darted to Abigail. A small smile played about her lips.

"Take a place on the bench," Abigail instructed, "and Tituba will tell us a story. Won't you?" She stepped to the worktable, picked up the kettle, and set it down in the middle of the kitchen table. Tituba, knife in hand, moved, too.

"I tell you this story," she began. "It be a true story that happened when my mother be just a child in Barbados. There was a young girl, very pretty girl, and she loved a young man. Her father, though, he be wealthy and the young man be poor."

"What happened?" demanded Abigail. "Did they get married?"

Tituba held out a hand, palm up. "Don't rush Tituba," she said. "If you want to hear the story, you must be patient." Abigail nodded, and she poked Ann and me who sat on either side of her in the ribs to signal that we, too, should nod. I was glad to do so. Listening to this story felt better than I imagined it would feel to ask Tituba questions for Mistress Putnam.

"Well, then," said Tituba. She paused, closed her eyes, and turned her face to the ceiling. "What happened? I tell you what happen. Something very sad happen. The boy, he tell the beautiful girl, sneak out to meet me tonight. We ride together on my horse to some other place, someplace where we marry and be happy." She stopped talking and took several whacks with her knife on the large piece of deer meat. We waited. "Well, it be a rainy night, that night they meet. They not know that father, he hear about plan and he wait for boy behind tree. When boy come, father step out with a gun. But girl jump in front."

"Oh," said Ann, "did he shoot her, his own daughter?"

Tituba, her face solemn, nodded slowly. "He kill her with his gun. The boy run and run—and get away—but father he kill his ownself, too." She made a clucking sound with her tongue. "The people around there, they hear the sound of girl crying, crying whenever it rain."

"Her ghost? It's the girl's ghost that cries, isn't it?" Abigail leaned across the table to look closely into the woman's eyes.

Tituba did not have a chance to answer because Ann blurted out, "My mother sees ghosts in her dreams sometimes. She sees the ghosts of my dead brothers and sisters, and sometimes her sister, too." She took a deep breath, then went on. "They talk to her, but she cannot understand most of their words."

"That be sad," said the woman. "Tituba she can see the sadness in your mother. The very first day I see her when I bring in the tea." She nodded slowly. "Ah, yes, I see the sadness."

I swallowed hard, then asked, "What do you suppose those dead babies say? Can you tell us what they may want to tell their mother?"

Deep in thought, Tituba twisted her face. "These dreams, do they leave the mother content, glad to have seen her babies?"

"No," said Ann. "Mother always wakes screaming. We've heard her scream about the dream many times, have we not, Drucilla?"

Tituba turned to me and after I nodded Tituba said, "She not happy, not glad to see her babies. They most likely tell her why they die."

"But how can we know the exact words?" I asked.

"Only the woman can know what they say. She must listen better." She paused, closed her eyes again, obviously getting more information. "Ah, no, 'tis too bad," she said after a bit, and she opened her eyes.

"What? What did you see?" Abigail leaned across the table to pull at Tituba's arm.

"Tituba not going to say," said the woman.

Something inside me whispered to me that I should get up and leave the kitchen. I should go and pull Ann with me. I should go home and tell Mistress Putnam that we had learned nothing. I looked at the door, then back at the other girls and Tituba.

Ann Putnam got up and walked around the table. She put her arm around the woman's waist and leaned against her. "Please, Tituba," she whispered. "Please tell us what you know of the dead babies."

Tituba sighed deeply. "God help us," she said. "I see those babies be murdered."

"That is exactly what my mother believes. Can you tell us who has done this horrible thing to our family?" Ann begged.

Just then Betty Parris screamed, a shrill and terrible sound, then she fainted, falling across the table.

Tituba rushed to pick the frail child up in her arms. "I take her to her bed," she said to the others. "Abigail you fetch water to her." She looked back at Ann and me, her dark eyes cold and angry. "You two go on home now." She used her head to point toward the door. "You tell no one what Tituba say."

Just outside the door, we paused. Snow had begun to fall again, but we ignored the flakes hitting our cloaks and faces. "What are we going to tell Mama?" Ann asked.

"We must tell her nothing yet. We can tell her that Betty fainted from fright after one of Tituba's stories and that ended our visit. I want to find out more before we start repeating things." I looked over my shoulder at the parsonage. "I don't know if I believe Tituba has special powers. She may tell her stories for sport."

"Oh, no." said Ann, "Tituba does know things." She shuddered. "Surely you could feel her power. When she spoke, something tingled all the way to my toes." She reached out to grab my wrist. "Tituba might be able to tell us who has caused Mama such pain." She tossed her head so that the hood of her cloak slipped off. "Mayhap you have no wish to help find out who torments Mama, but I do."

"I do," I said. "I want to be more certain, that's all."

The next day Abigail came early to the kitchen door to tell Ann that her aunt was unwell and would be home all day. I was greatly relieved.

Chapter Nine

The events with Tituba had haunted me all the previous day and were still very much on my mind. I thought a walk might help clear my head, and, of course, I was always eager to see Gabe. I had no intention of talking about what was on my mind, and I suggested a game of draughts. "What's wrong with you?" Gabe asked when he had jumped three of my men and I crowned his men kings without protest. "You're not thinking about this game."

I closed my eyes for a moment. "I am unwell," I said, and I spoke no lie. I had been unable to sleep the night before, and my head whirled with fears. "I think I should not have come." I stood.

Gabe got up, too. "What troubles you?"

I sighed. "Mayhap I am coming down with a cold from being out yesterday while the snow fell."

"Wait for me. I'll get the horse and cart. I don't want you walking back."

We talked but little on the ride. Gabe took a heavy blanket from a wooden box on the back of the cart and wrapped it about me. It was most unfortunate that just as we stopped in front of the

Putnam house, young Ann came out the front door. When she saw us, she hurried in our direction. I started at once to climb down, but so did Gabe.

"Drucilla," Ann called, "I am glad you are back. Betty and Abigail have invited us to come for a cup of tea," she said nothing more until she stood beside us, and I knew she had used the moment for thinking. "They are working on new samplers and are most anxious for us to see them."

"I am not well," I told her. "You go on without me."

Ann reached for my hand and pulled it. "We will only stay a bit. Tituba can make her special tea for you while we look at the samplers. Then we will leave."

I looked over my shoulder and saw Mistress Putnam. She had opened the front door and stood looking in our direction. I knew she would insist I go if I came to her door. "Maybe the tea would make me feel better," I said.

"You go on, Ann," Gabe said, and he came to stand beside me. "Drucilla will be there in a moment."

Ann hesitated. I knew she did not want to leave without me, but I also knew she was awfully fond of Gabe and did not want to appear disagreeable in front of him. "Very well, but don't be long. I'll tell Tituba to make the tea, and you should have it hot."

"Who is Tituba?" Gabe asked.

"The Parrises' slave woman, and they have a man, John Indian. Reverend Parris sometimes hires him out to work at Ingersoll's Ordinary. They brought the couple with them from Barbados."

"All he had left of his failed business, I'll wager, but I have a small gift for you. I suppose you could say that I, too, have made a sampler. Give me your hand," he said.

I held out my hand and he put a small square of wood into it. It had been smoothed and polished, and letters were carved into it. I saw the word "Genesis," and knew it was a Bible verse, but before I had a chance to read it, Gabe spoke.

"It says 'The Lord watch between me and thee when we are absent one from the other,' from a Bible verse in Genesis."

If I should live to be a very, very old lady, the memory of that moment will, I believe, still be fresh and alive for me. I remember the sound of the horse snorting. I remember Gabe's dear voice and the pressure of his hand on mine. I remember the fear that leaped inside me. "Do you think we will be parted, then?"

"Sometimes," he said, "I am afraid we have already begun to be. I am worried about you. Something is wrong, and you aren't telling me. Not really. Since when do we have secrets from each other?"

I could not speak. I leaned my head against his chest for only a second, but knowing it was not proper to do so, I pulled away. "Don't be a goose," I managed to say. "I will treasure your gift always, but I must go to drink my tea." I began to move quickly toward the Parris house.

"Good-bye, Dru," he called. "Be careful."

How did he know I felt afraid? Gabe seemed often almost to read my mind. I slipped the little plaque into my pocket, turned in his direction, and waved, but I did not let my eyes truly focus. Had I actually looked at him, I might have run toward him instead of toward the Parris home.

Ann, already at the Parrises' door, waited for me. "I am so glad you are here. Mother will be pleased also," she said before she knocked. "Abigail just came to say her aunt's headache was better and that she had gone out with the minister. I was going on without you when you came."

Abigail let us into the house. Tituba was there, sitting in the rocking chair before the fire with a basket of mending at her feet. She looked up and frowned when she saw us. "Ah, it is just as well you turn back at once and go home if you come here to pester Tituba for stories." She held up a petticoat with a rip clearly visible. "Tituba got work to do. No time for foolish girls today."

Abigail shoved Betty slightly toward Tituba. We all knew Betty was Tituba's favorite. "Please," Betty said. "Please tell Abigail's fortune. You said you would soon."

Tituba sighed and put down the petticoat. "Last time my stories scare you, remember?"

Betty turned slightly to glance at Abigail, who shot back a look and a small wave of her hand. "No," said Betty in a soft voice. "I fainted because I felt suddenly dizzy. It had nothing to do with your story. Please now look at Abigail's hand."

Tituba sighed again. "Very well, but just this one thing before I go back to work." She motioned toward Abigail. "You, girl, come to Tituba, and hold out your hand."

Abigail's face came alive with excitement. "Tell me," she said at once. "What do you see?"

Tituba made a sort of huffing sound. "I see a little miss who is too impatient."

"I'm sorry." Abigail ducked her head. "I'll be still until you are ready."

Tituba grunted. She held Abigail's hand close to her face. Finally, she spoke. "I see much happiness for you, a fine young man to marry." She leaned even closer to the hand. "Ah, I see wealth."

"Really?"

"Yes, I am sure of it. And babies! You will have beautiful babies."

"Babies," said Ann. "Last time you told us that my mother's babies were murdered. Can you tell us who killed them?"

Tituba's eyes darted quickly to little Betty. She dropped Abigail's hand and lifted the torn petticoat from her lap. "I not talk of murder. Not today."

Abigail kicked lightly at the smaller girl's leg. "It's all right," said Betty. "You can talk about murdered babies. I am not afraid." Her face, though, looked terrified.

"No," said Tituba, "but we do something much better. You girlies like to see the face of the man you marry, yes?"

"Yes, oh, yes!" shouted Abigail.

"Fetch me egg. Be careful. The mistress, she notice if we use more than one." Abigail ran to a cabinet, and Tituba heaved her bulk from the chair and moved to stand beside the table. "Betty, you dip glass of water from bucket."

"What now?" Abigail asked, and she placed the egg in Tituba's hand.

"You push too much, too many questions. You be still and watch." Tituba took the glass from Betty. She cracked the egg against the rim of the glass and dropped just the egg white into the water. Placing the glass beside a candle, she peered into it, rolled her eyes, and muttered, "Ah, 'tis ready." She looked from one girl to the next and spoke in a low voice. "If you look hard into glass, you might see the face of man you are to marry."

Abigail and Ann squealed with delight. Abigail looked first. "Oh, I can! I can see his nose and the way his hair grows on his head."

"Do you know him?" Ann asked, and she reached for the glass.

"I don't know." Abigail turned so that Ann could not take the glass. "Let me look longer. I must be ready to recognize him when we meet."

Ann, though, would not be put off. She walked around the table, snatched the glass from Abigail, held it near the candle, looked in, and squealed. "I know him! I do. Let me think! Oh, I know, it's Gabe Matson. Just think, Drucilla, I am to marry your old friend! Isn't that amazing?"

Tituba reached for the glass. "Maybe you don't see right. Give glass to Drucilla."

I did not want to take the glass. I shook my head, but Tituba reached for my hand and placed the glass in it. "Look, now, dearie," she said.

I did as I was told. "I don't see anything except an egg white," I said.

"Well," said Abigail, "maybe you won't marry at all. Some women never do."

"Don't worry," said Ann, "after Mother and Father die, you can live with me and Gabe." There was no meanness in her voice, but I said nothing.

"Betty," said Abigail, "it's your turn."

The little girl backed away. "I don't want to look," she said. "Don't make me."

Tituba went to Betty and put an arm around her. "Nobody make you do anything you no want to do, baby. You no need to fret. Tituba make a pie now. Company go home, and you and cousin study the scripture. Father, he said have it on memory when he get back, remember?"

"I'll get the Bibles," said Betty, and she ran to the shelf near the fire. "I almost have mine. Come, Abigail, we must do as Father says."

"Company go now. Shoo, neighbors, go back to your place." She waved her hands at Ann and me, then pointed to Abigail and Betty. "These ones got work to do."

"I'll walk with you just a little," said Abigail, and she grabbed her cloak from a peg. Outside she took one of my arms and one of Ann's. "Oh, on the morrow we shall have a delight. Aunt and Uncle go to Andover to see a sick friend they knew in Boston. They leave before first light." She smiled broadly. "We will have the day, the whole day." She lowered her voice. "Mayhap I will also invite some others to come and join us."

I frowned. "Who? It is not safe to let just anyone know what we do here."

Abigail tossed her head. "Oh, Drucilla, you two aren't the only ones who have been here to visit with Tituba. Didn't Ann tell you?" She held up her hand and began to count off names. "Let me see. We've had Mary Walcott, Mary Warren, Susannah Sheldon, and Mercy Lewis." She laughed. "I think every one of them has mentioned the name of another girl who wants to come along. We may have quite a large group. It will be jolly."

I looked down and began to use one of my shoes to draw lines in the snow. "No, Ann did not tell me there were others. I do not like it. Groups can't keep secrets."

"Don't be such a worrier," Ann said, and for the first time in three years she reached out for my hand as if we were comrades.

"That's right," said Abigail. "Let me do the worrying. After all, it is Betty and I who would be in the most trouble should the word get out. We are the ones who live with His Majesty the Reverend."

Ann and I did not talk on the short walk back home. We found Mistress Putnam waiting for us in the kitchen. She got up from her chair when she saw us. "Come upstairs with me," she said. When we had followed her into her chamber, she closed the door. "I do not trust Rose Thatcher," she said. She sat down on the bed and patted places on either side of her. "Come tell, did you learn anything today?"

Ann clapped her hands. "Oh, yes, we learned that I will marry Gabe Matson and that Drucilla may never marry." She leaned against her mother and hugged her. "On the morrow we will have the whole day with Tituba, uninterrupted."

Mistress Putnam moved Ann's arms, got up, and began to

pace about the room. "This is good news, but we must learn more. I want to know if my husband's wealth will be greater than our neighbors'. I want to know about Joseph Putnam and about the Nurse family. The Nurses will have as much land as we do if they continue to make payment on those acres beside ours. That land should belong to us, but they are buying it with yearly payments." She stopped walking, put her hands on my shoulders, and looked directly into my eyes. "You have said nothing, my dear. Is there something you are not telling me?"

I felt my face growing hot, but Ann spoke, causing her mother to whirl to look in her direction. "We found out something yesterday, but Drucilla said we shouldn't tell you."

"About what? Tell me!" Mistress Putnam reached for Ann's arm and jerked it.

I thought she looked as if she might hit Ann. I spoke quickly. "I was afraid you would be too upset if we told you. It's about the babies."

Mistress Putnam drew in a deep breath. "Tell me," she demanded.

"Tituba said your babies were murdered," Ann said, and I wondered at the sound of delight in her voice. How could she be so glad to deliver such terrible news? Then I understood. Ann was delighted because she knew her mother would be pleased with this terrible news.

"I knew it! Now that we have proof, we must find the person who has caused this terrible slaughter and see the murderer punished." Her eyes blazed and she held out her hands in a stopping sign. "Nay, I should not say person! This is too big a thing to have been caused by one person! I must say persons. They conspire against us." She went to the window and stared out. "Even now they are out there, plotting hideous things against us! They must be stopped."

I rose from my place on the bed and went to stand beside her. "But we don't have real proof of murder. We have only a comment made by a slave woman seeking to entertain girls. That isn't proof, is it?"

Mistress Putnam took me by the shoulders. Her eyes were glowing with excitement. "Yes, oh, yes, child. I have known my babies to be the victim of those who hate me, known for a long time. This woman, Tituba, sees things, and she has confirmed my belief." She moved one of her hands to my cheek. "A mother can sense these things, dear Drucilla. A mother feels the truth when her babies are attacked. Do you not believe me? Say you do."

I loved the touch of her hand. I wanted desperately to help her, wanted to keep her as an active part of our lives. "I do, of course, Mother. I believe you." I meant it, too, at the time. I made a conscious decision to push myself into believing whatever she said, and I know now that it was at that moment I began to descend into darkness.

Chapter Ten

For the rest of the day, Mistress Putnam sang quietly to herself as she went about her work. Young Ann shared her mother's good mood. "I wish night would hurry," she said. "When we go to bed, it will be no time until we go to the party."

I said nothing, only bent to put my arm around little Thomas. "Would you like me to tell you a story?" I asked, but he was busy with his carving.

"You aren't happy about the morrow?" Ann stopped stacking the dishes from the evening meal, left the table, and came to stand beside me near the window. "Tell me why. Why do you not look forward to hearing Tituba?"

I shrugged my shoulders. "We shouldn't dabble in such matters. We will but invite evil into our lives."

"Don't be such a baby. What could happen? Besides, it makes Mother happy. You do want Mother to be happy, do you not?"

I could only nod. I moved to the spinning wheel. Flax needed to be spun into thread. I would work at the wheel all evening, but as I fastened the strips of flax to the distaff, making ready to turn the wheel and begin making the flax into threads that would become linen, I fretted over what would happen the next day.

That night I could not rest. When Ann's regular breathing

indicated that she was asleep, I slipped from our bed and went downstairs to the great hall to stand beside a window. The white stones stood out in the moonlight. For a long time I stared at the graves and remembered the feeling of holding the dead baby in my arms. Could it be true that someone had caused the death of that sweet angel by putting a curse on her mother? Mistress Putnam believed so strongly. Shouldn't I do all that I could do to determine the truth? Yes, I was certain I should make every effort. Why, then, did I feel this terrible dread? I began to shake with cold, and I went back up to bed.

Ann woke me early the next morning. "Get up, Drucilla. Our big day has come. We must breakfast quickly and make ready for going to the Parrises'. Abigail says we are to bring something for our noontide meal. If we were all to eat from the Parrises' kitchen, the food would be missed and our visit discovered."

Mistress Putnam came into the room while we were dressing. "Now, you must be whisht and mum about your plans for the day. Your father is to know nothing, nor Rose neither. Come, Ann, let me tie your sash."

"Ye be up and about some early," said Rose when we came down to the kitchen. She turned to look directly at Ann. "And something be stirring. I can see it in ye faces, I can."

"We are to spend the day at the parsonage," I said.

"Yes," Ann jumped in. "Drucilla is to teach Abigail and Betty to spin. I'm to learn, too."

Amazed by the quickness with which Ann lied and by how unconcerned she was with the sin of lying, I turned to set wooden bowls on the table. "Spinning class, huh?" Rose laughed. "Seems to me lots of classes have come to be held at the Reverend's house." She laughed again. "I hear things, ye know, and I am wondering does the Reverend Parris know about these classes?" She took the kettle from the fire, set it on the table, and began to dip porridge into the bowls.

"I am sure the Reverend has far too much to do to stay attuned to activities and entertainments of mere girls," I said, and I began to slice bread.

Rose made a huffing sound. "More's the pity, I say. The good Reverend needs to look to his own house first."

Mistress Putnam appeared then with little Thomas and Elizabeth. "Stop the talking, Rose, and get these children fed."

While Ann ate her breakfast, I cut pieces of cheese and bread and wrapped them in a clean cloth for our lunch. I refused the porridge Mistress Putnam urged on me. "I'd rather not eat," I said. "My stomach is a bit unsettled."

Mistress Putnam came to me and touched my cheek. "No fever. You are just excited about a holiday at the Parris home. Away with you now, and have a good time."

Ann took her cloak from the peg and had it on before I could cross the room. "Hurry," she whispered when I was beside her. "We mustn't miss anything." She pulled on my arm.

It was a dreary day. No sun came through the snow clouds that dumped big flakes on us as we walked. A light shone from the window of the Parris house, and I kept my eye on it as we walked. Near the house, I saw sets of prints in the snow on the stone walk that led to the kitchen door. I pointed out the prints to Ann. "Abigail said others might come. Someone had best make sure those prints aren't visible when we leave. The Reverend is sure to notice."

Betty came to the door to answer the knock. "Come in," she said, and she offered us a weak smile. Her face looked white, and I felt sorry for the little girl, who was being forced by her strong-minded cousin to participate in an activity that scared her.

Five village girls crowded around the table with Betty and Abigail. I knew them all. They were older than me, five to eight years older than Abigail. I thought it odd that they were eager enough to hear Tituba's stories that they would come early on so dreary a morning and be directed by Abigail, a much younger girl.

"Tell us about witches," Mary Warren was saying as Ann and I came in. "Did you have witches in Barbados?"

"Ah, yes," said Tituba, and the pleased sound in her voice was easy to hear. "We had witches many, just as here, too." She left her place, and pulling herself up to her full height, she spread her hands, fingers wide above the table. "In Barbados we no keep witches alive. We burn them, all tied up. Once when I am little girl I see witch burned, but I see her float off above her body." She shook her head. "Ah, she no die. She come back and make people who hurt her very sick till they die."

"I know about a witch in Boston," Elizabeth Hubbard said, and we all leaned forward. "She was a washerwoman named Glover." Her voice dropped low, and the listeners barely breathed in order to hear every word. "I don't remember her first name, but it does not matter because everyone called her Witch Glover. That was, of course, after she did her terrible mischief. She worked for a good man and his family. His name was John Goodwin, and he did not know that the woman he hired to work in his home was a witch. John Goodwin and his wife had four children. They were healthy and well behaved, never laughed during prayers and studied the scripture every day, but after Witch Glover came into the house, they went wild. They barked like dogs and bit one another most grievously." She stopped and breathed a long, loud sigh.

"What happened?" asked Mary Walcott. "Tell us what happened."

"Well, they killed her of course. Don't you know the Bible says 'Thou shall not suffer a witch to live'?"

"Did they burn her at the stake?" asked Mary Warren.

Elizabeth shook her head. "No, witches can't be burned anymore, not in England or in English colonies, anyway. They hanged her. My mother says that if we had known in time we would have gone to see Witch Glover dangle from the tree because it is good for children to see what becomes of people who break God's law."

"So were the children all right after the witch was dead?" asked Susannah Sheldon.

"Not at first. There is a famous preacher in Boston named Cotton Mather. He had to spend many days working with the afflicted children before they could throw off their strange behavior."

"My mother says there is much evil in Salem," said Ann, "and that our family has been injured by all the secret evil."

"And can you tell us why doth your mother have so much knowledge of hidden things?" asked Mercy Lewis, and the irritation in her voice was plain.

Ann flashed Mercy an indignant look. "My mother has six dead babies! Do you know yet another woman with so many dead children?" She paused and looked at each face. "I thought not. When a woman has that many dead babies, it makes her special. She knows things."

"Let's not talk of witches anymore," said Mary Warren, and she gave herself a bit of a shake. "It makes me feel odd. Besides, I want to know about suitors. I am twenty and have no young man calling."

Ann smiled widely. "I saw the face of the man I will marry yesterday in Tituba's egg. I am to wed Gabriel Matson!"

The girls laughed. "You are mistaken," said Mercy Lewis. "Everyone in the village knows Drucilla will marry Gabe Matson."

I felt my face grow hot. "We have never spoken of marriage," I said quietly.

"You've no need to speak of it," said Elizabeth Hubbard. "I know. I tried my hand at getting Gabe to notice me, tried for at least a year before I gave up." She rolled her eyes. "He is yours, all right."

"We shall see," said Ann, and she folded her arms across her chest.

"I brought two eggs from Elizabeth Proctor's kitchen," said Mary Warren. "The stingy thing will likely beat me if she notices they are gone. I hate that woman." She reached into the pocket of her dress and took out the eggs, wrapped in cloth.

"I get the water," said Tituba, but she did not move because Abigail shook her head to stop her.

"We saw Witch Glover hanged in Boston," Abigail announced. Her voice was clear and strong, and yet there was a sound to it, almost as if she said the words in a dream. Every eye turned toward her. "Do you not remember, Betty? We were living in Boston then before we went to Barbados. I was five, and you were three. Perhaps you were too young to have a memory of it, but I remember clearly, every detail."

"Tell us about it," said Ann.

Abigail closed her eyes for a moment, but the group waited in total silence. "She wore a dress so faded that it looked almost white. Her feet and hands were bound. A big man threw her over his shoulder and climbed up a ladder. He fastened a rope around her neck, and he asked her if she wanted to speak. 'I am innocent,' she said, 'and God will punish you all for taking my life, even those who came to see me die for sport, you, too, will be punished.' I remember I felt very strange, and I hid behind Aunt's skirts. The man pushed her then, and she swung from the tree. She had on only one shoe. What do you suppose became of her other shoe?" Then she turned to Betty again. "Are you sure you have no memory of the hanging?"

"No," said Betty, "I do not remember. Mayhap I did not attend. I may have been ill from a fever that day." She looked down at the table. "I was often ill when we lived in Boston."

"I don't believe you," said Abigail. "I can tell by the look of you that you do remember. You're just afraid to talk about it." Her expression was full of disgust. "You are such a baby."

Tituba got up and filled two glasses with water. Mary Warren took up one of the eggs, cracked it against the rim, dropped the egg white into the water, and moved the glass to sit beside the candle. "I mean to have the first look," she said, and she moved her head low over the glass. "I think I can see a face," she said after a moment of close scrutiny, "but I wouldn't have a man with so long a nose."

Mary Walcott laughed. "You're the oldest of us all," she said. "It would be my opinion that if ever a man asks, you had best say yes, long nose or no."

Mary Warren made a face at Mary Walcott and slid the glass across the table. "What see you, Susannah?"

"Nothing. Mayhap each girl must use a different egg." Susannah shrugged her shoulders. "I'd rather talk of witches, anyway."

Tituba shot a glance at Betty, who still looked down at the table. "My master does not like talk of witches."

"Your master," said Abigail, "would just as quickly thrash you for telling our fortunes."

Tituba shook her head. "No more witch talk to make my Betty afraid."

"Tituba is always overworried about her precious Betty," Abigail said to the other girls as if Tituba could not hear her. She went to stand behind where Betty sat on the bench. "Tell her you want to hear stories about witches." Abigail's thumb thumped hard into Betty's back.

"I am not afraid, Tituba," said Betty, but her face looked pale.

"Come on, please, Tituba," said Ann. "I have questions to ask you about witches. My mother says you are a wise woman."

Tituba smiled. "Ah, yes," she said. "There is much I could tell you."

"What do witches do?" asked Ann.

"Curses, of course." Tituba spread out her arms and moved her hands slowly over the table and benches. "I know a witch once, here some man has a cow, she die. There a woman, her hair all come out."

"Did she ever cause a death?" asked Ann.

Tituba nodded several times. "She cause many deaths." Her voice dropped to little more than a whisper. "She have this cat. It take away much breath from babies in that village, and children, even. Pretty little ones with rosy cheeks and bright eyes when they go to bed. They no wake up in morning."

"How was she discovered?" asked Susannah.

"Ah, a little girl she see the witchy woman with a big yellow bird, and it feed from between her fingers. Blood! She give the bird her blood. Blood drip from between the witch's fingers."

Ann pushed herself up from the bench by putting her hands on the table. "So they burned her because of what one girl saw?" Ann leaned toward Tituba.

"Many others come forward after the girl told about the bird. Many people, all tell."

"Goody Nurse has a yellow bird," said Abigail. "I have seen it."

"It is but a parrot brought back by one of her sons who went to sea," I said quickly. "It does not drink blood."

"Do you think there are witches in Salem Village? You know, witches we don't know about?" asked Ann.

Tituba leaned low over the table. She looked once over her shoulder before she spoke in a low whisper. "Witches be everywhere. Good Christian people not know where to look." She looked from face to face. “You girlies, you stay close with Tituba. Tituba know how to protect you.”

At noontide each girl ate the food she had brought with her. Tituba filled wooden trenchers with stew for Betty and Abigail. Betty ate but little. “My stomach feels unwell,” she told Tituba, who inquired as to why she had no appetite.

Tituba touched Betty’s forehead. “No fever,” she said, relieved.

“Here,” said Abigail, “I’ll eat your stew.” She reached across the table, drew Betty’s trencher to her place, and scraped the food from the wooden plate onto her own. She began to eat, but when Tituba went outside for firewood to fill the box beside the hearth, Abigail spoke to Betty. “Stop being such a baby.” She sighed and frowned. “She’s not unwell,” she said to the other girls. “She’s just afraid, that’s all, and if she doesn’t stop it, Tituba won’t tell us any more stories or let us look at egg whites or anything else.” She made a disgusted sound. She pointed her finger at her cousin and shook it. “It’s a warning I am giving you. You get yourself unafraid or all of us will give you something to really be afraid of.”

“But Father,” Betty’s voice quivered, “he would be most angry if he knew. He would say we were committing sins. You know he would.”

Abigail shrugged her shoulders. “Maybe so. Sin is all Uncle Samuel seems to think on, but how is he to know?” She reached across the table to grab roughly at Betty’s arm. “You had best not tell him, Betty. If you do, you will be in as much trouble as any of us. That is all I have to say. If you don’t tell, your father will never know.” Abigail gritted her teeth and nodded her head.

Betty swallowed hard, and her blue eyes grew large. “I would never tell. I promise.”

“Very well,” said Abigail. “When Tituba comes back in, tell her you will eat some stew.” She took Betty’s arm again and twisted it until the smaller girl cried out.

"I will," she whimpered.

"Tell her you feel better, and that you want to hear more stories."

"I will, Abby, just don't be mad at me."

The door opened just then, and Tituba, her arms full of wood, came in. "Do it," Abigail said under her breath, and she slid Betty's empty trencher across the table.

"I feel better now, Tituba," Betty said, and I thought she sounded convincing. "I'll just get myself some stew." She started to rise from her place on the bench.

"No." Tituba dropped the wood into the box and held out her hand to stop Betty. "Kettle too big for little girl. Tituba get her angel some stew." She took the trencher, filled it, and brought it back to the table.

"Eat it." Abigail mouthed the words, and Betty, eyes down, began.

"We still have one egg to drop," said Susannah Sheldon. "I've just thought of the peddler who came to our place a few nights ago. He was young and handsome. It seemed to me that he fancied me. Perhaps I will try the glass after all. Mary, may I please have the last egg?"

Mary handed Susannah the egg and Abigail supplied the water. "You have to believe," she said. "Magic won't work if you don't believe. Is that not so, Tituba?"

"You speak the truth," said Tituba.

"It is the peddler!" shouted Susannah. "I wonder when he shall return for me." She began to hum softly under her breath.

"Tituba," said Abigail, "the girls will need to go home soon. Tell us one last story about witches."

"No." Tituba shook her head. "My Betty, she afraid of such stories." She turned from the table toward the hearth.

Under the table, I felt Abigail's leg move to give Betty a kick. "I'm not," said Betty. "I love your stories. Please."

"Well then, I tell you about that witch in Boston. I not live with this family then. I still back in my Barbados, but I hear about woman, named Glover. I hear from woman who speak only truth, my mistress, minister's wife. She tell me shush." Tituba put her fingers to her lips. "She tell me my master, he no like talk of witch magic in the house."

"What did you learn about Witch Glover?" Mary Warren asked.

"I learn she hurt those children. She pinch them and bite them, and they not act right. They no talk, just make sounds like animals."

"Why? Why would she do that?" I asked the question loudly, and the others looked at me because I was so loud and also because I was usually fairly quiet.

"Why she do that?" Tituba tilted her head and stared at me. I could see that she was thinking. She began to nod her head. "Ah, yes, she do it because she work for devil! Ah, yes, devil he like to make people suffer. He tell her to hurt children."

"What does Satan look like, Tituba?" asked Ann.

Tituba made a face. "Oh, Tituba never see that awful man. Tituba not know what he looks like. If ever you see him, you look other way and run."

Abigail had risen to stand near a window. "I am afraid my uncle and aunt may return soon." She waved her hand in our direction. "You had best go, all of you, and tell no one what we have talked of this day." She took up a broom, followed the group from the house, and spread snow over our footprints.

Chapter Eleven

Mistress Putnam had been watching for us, and she met us outside. "Did you discover who has cursed us?" She looked back at the house as she spoke. "Your father has come in early from his labors because of an ache in his knee. I do not wish him to hear us talk." She reached out to take our arms and draw us to either side of her.

"We learned nothing of a curse," I said, and I saw a pained look cross Mistress Putnam's face.

"We will, though, I am sure of it. There will be other days," said Ann.

"Yes," I assured her. "We will seek more information."

She smiled then, and putting her arms across our shoulders, she hugged us close.

"How fortunate I am to have two such fine daughters who want to protect me." She let go of us and walked toward the door. "Come. We have chores to do."

That evening after everyone else was asleep, I went down to the kitchen for a drink of water. The bucket was empty, and my mouth was too dry to wait until morning. I went to the peg to get my cloak. When I turned back, Rose sat up on her pallet before the kitchen hearth.

"I should have filled the bucket before." She stood up and reached to take the bucket from my hand.

"I'll draw the water," I told her. "I've my cloak already."

"The mistress won't like it," she said.

"No need to mention the water to her," I said, and headed for the door. Outside the sky was bright with stars, and the moon, round and full, seemed to hang just over the well. I had pulled the bucket almost all the way up when the scream split the silent night. Startled, I almost lost my hold on the rope. The scream came again, and I realized it had come from the Parris home. I saw a light through the window of an upstairs chamber where I knew Betty and Abigail slept. I emptied the water from the well bucket quickly into the pail I had brought from the house. So hurried was I that I spilled water on the part of my nightgown that stuck out beneath the bottom of my cloak. My leg felt cold against the wet fabric, but I little noticed because the scream came again, a terrible fear-filled sound that made me shiver far more than did the cold night.

Rose had come to stand in the open doorway. "What was that?" she asked when I was close. "I thought I heard something before, too."

"Someone is screaming at the minister's house," I said. "Three times I heard it."

Rose stepped back so that I could enter, but she did not close the door. Instead she walked out onto the back stoop. The scream came again. Rose came back inside and closed the door, sliding the wooden bolt across it. "Gives me a fright, that sound. Who do you suppose is screaming like that?"

My mouth was full of the drink I had sought. I shook my head. When I had swallowed I said, "I have no idea." It was a lie. The screamer was little Betty Parris. I was certain of that, but, like Rose, I was bothered greatly by the sound and had no wish to discuss it. I remembered Betty's pale face and the fear in her big blue eyes. Was she even now pouring it all out to her parents? Did they know now what had been happening in their kitchen? If so, there would be a great deal of punishment going on in that house, probably tonight. The Reverend Parris did not strike me as a man who would put off beatings until daylight.

At breakfast, Rose related the story about the screams. "Drucilla came down for a drink, she did, just when I had realized the pail be empty. I was going for the water when the screaming started. Drucilla heard it, too." She looked at me, "Didn't ye?"

"I did," I said. "I looked out and saw a light in the chamber where Betty and Abigail sleep. It must have been one of them, likely Betty."

Mistress Putnam went on filling the bowls with porridge, but I could see the look of concern on her face. "I'd best go to the Parrises' after we eat. If there is trouble there, I may be of some help," she said.

When breakfast was over, I did not spend the morning as I often did teaching young Thomas his lessons. I decided to work at the spinning wheel, where I could look out the window and see the Parris house. It was hard to keep my mind on my work. I turned constantly watching always for Mistress Putnam.

At last she did return. Ann and I both ran to her. "Let us go up to my chamber," she said.

"Is it a secret, then?" Rose turned from the kettle she had been tending and stared at us. "Am I not to know the cause of the screaming? It was me that told ye of it!"

Mistress Putnam gave Rose a scornful look. "The screams were nothing, only a girl's bad dreams. There is nothing to be kept secret. I wish to discuss other matters with my daughters. I hope it is not necessary for me to ask your permission to do so.

See to our noon meal." She stomped out of the room. Ann and I followed. Rose stood staring angrily after us.

Upstairs Mistress Putnam closed the door to her chamber. "Over here," she said, "away from the door in case Rose tries to listen." Ann and I sat on the bed, but Mistress Putnam stood. "Betty Parris is ill," she said, her voice very soft. "Last night she woke the family with screams, but she could not speak of what frightened her. She has said nothing this morning, only stares off into space."

"What does her father say?" I asked.

"He wants her to fast and to spend her time in prayer."

"Not eating won't help her," I said. "She is frightened by the stories Tituba told us and by her knowledge that her father would be furious if he knew about the fortune-telling and the witch talk."

"Let us hope she does not tell what has been happening." Mistress Putnam closed her mouth hard and gritted her teeth. "If the minister does discover what has been going on, he will likely come here to question you both." She moved over to stand in front of us, leaning to take hold of one of each of our arms. "Should that happen, you must not tell him that I urged you to go. You are but young and can be forgiven your interest in the black arts. Reverend Parris would think me evil if he knew I had urged you to question the woman."

"We would never betray you, Mother," said Ann.

"Drucilla?" Mistress Putnam removed her hand from Ann's arm and placed it on my free one.

A chill went through my body, but I forced my voice to sound normal. "Of course not, Mother. I would never do anything to hurt you," I said.

Right after the noontide meal, Mistress Putnam made a hasty pudding for our evening meal. "I've made extra," she said, "enough for the Parris family." She looked from me to Ann. I knew she was deciding who should take the gift across the street, and I dearly hoped I would not be selected. Ann had an eager look about her, but it was I who was sent.

"I think Ann would like to go," I said when Mistress Putnam announced that I should be the carrier. "Could she not take it instead?"

The woman shook her head. "No, I think this is a job for my older daughter. You may be able to observe something we need to know."

With each step through the snow, my dread grew. I was barely able to make myself knock at the door. I had gone to the front door, thinking that I would not have to see Tituba. Abigail answered. "Betty's acting up," she whispered when I had stepped inside, "letting on that she is in some kind of trance. I've told her that she'd best get hold of herself. She's playing with fire. We could all be in a lot of trouble."

Just then the minister's wife came into the great hall. "My mother sent this hasty pudding," I said, and I held out the wooden bowl.

She took the bowl. "How kind of her to want to ease our hard days with a sweet." She started to turn away, and then thought better of it. "Won't you come into the kitchen and say hello to our Betty? I am afraid she may not speak to you, but mayhap she will find pleasure in seeing you." I followed her through the kitchen door. Betty sat in front of the hearth. A Bible was in her lap, but she did not look down at it, only at the fire.

Tituba stood at the kitchen table kneading bread. She looked up at me, and I saw a warning there in her dark eyes. "Hello, Betty," I said. The little girl glanced away from the fire in my direction, but she said nothing.

The minister's wife came to stand beside me. "Do you not

wish to say hello to your friend?" she asked, but Betty's eyes had gone back to the blaze.

"We are so worried about her," said her mother. She reached out to stroke Betty's blond hair.

I studied the girl's blank face. I did not agree with Abigail. Betty was not acting up. I believed that her conscience and her fear had left her unable to cope, and I felt a terrible guilt for taking part in activities that made the little girl suffer so. "I wish I might help, but I do not know how," I said.

Her mother smiled a weary sort of smile. "Of course, you don't my dear. Neither do we know how to help." She set the bowl on the kitchen table. "Tell your mother I shall send Abigail over with the bowl when the pudding is gone, and tell her I said thank you."

"I'll just go out the back door," I said, and I moved quickly across the room. Just before closing the door behind me, I looked back. Betty sat absolutely still, staring into the fire.

That evening Gabe came to see me. "I've been worried about you," he said when I opened the door to him. "Do you feel better?"

It took me a moment to remember that I had claimed to be coming down with a cold. "Oh, yes," I said. 'I am fine now."

Gabe did not give me his cloak. "I'll just stay a moment," he said. "I have some news." At just that moment Ann came down the stairs.

"Oh, Gabe," she said. "No one told me you had come to call."

"It will be but a short visit," he said. "I've come only to see if Drucilla felt better."

She smiled at him adoringly. "Well, I hope you notice that there are others of us in this house as well."

I could see that Gabe did not know what to say. "I am sure he does," I said.

He turned to me. "I must be on my way, but I hope you will walk out with me. There's a matter to tell you about."

I turned to get my cloak. Ann moved for the door, ready to go out into the cold with no wrap at all. "I hope you won't mind," Gabe said to her, "but I have something I'd like to talk over with Drucilla in private."

An angry look passed over Ann's face, but when she spoke her voice was pleasant. "I'll forgive you this once," she smiled at him. "You must promise, though, to come back when you've time enough to tarry."

"What is the girl up to?" he asked when we were outside.

I laughed. "She has fallen in love with you. In fact she believes she saw your face in a glass of water with an egg white in it, meaning the two of you will wed."

Gabe groaned. "She'd best have another look. The day I would marry Ann Putnam's daughter will never come."

"You know I call her Mother sometimes," I said.

"I do, and I don't like it, Dru. You have had two mothers. One gave her life for you, and one loved you as her own. Do you not remember my mother? I can close my eyes and hear the song she sang to us at night. She loved you just as much as she did me. Even so young, I knew that. Why would you need Ann Putnam?"

"I am not as strong as you," I said. "I do need a mother, but her need for a daughter is even stronger. She needs me, Gabe, and I cannot deny that need." I bit at my lip a moment then went on. "People are often unkind to her. She thinks she has been cursed by her enemies."

"Her enemies? I know no one in Salem Village to fear except Ann Putnam. She draws you more and more into her illness. She is not cursed, Dru. She has suffered, yes, but so have others. The woman feeds on bitterness and discontent. She would have you feed at the same hateful table."

For a moment there was only silence between us, and we walked on. When we were beside the cart, I poked him in the ribs. "Tell me your news," I said.

"I am to go to school," he told me. "Mary Putnam is willing to pay my way through Harvard. I will start next fall. Is that not wonderful?"

I reached out to throw my arms around him in a celebratory hug. "It is what you've always wanted," I said, but I grew quickly self-conscious. In our early years together Gabe and I had touched each other easily, perhaps as bear cubs might have touched in play. Of late, though, our touching had been much less and had become awkward when it did occur. Besides, in that quick moment, I had realized what his announcement meant to me. Gabe would be going far away from Salem Village. He might never return here at all. He was leaving me. I tossed my head in defiance. He might warn me not to be close to Ann Putnam and her family, but he would not be here. Should I withdraw from my relationship with Mistress Putnam, there would be no Gabe Matson to stand with me. I took a step back from him.

"What's wrong, Dru? Are you not happy for me?"

"I shall miss you, that's all," I said. "We are to be truly separated for the first time in our lives."

"Cambridge is but a short distance from Salem Village. I will come back here every time the college has a holiday." He laughed. "Likely we will see each other almost as often as we do now." Suddenly his face became very serious, and, uncharacteristically, he reached out to touch my hand. "I will write to you, Drucilla, and you will answer just as Granny Morton told us. I could never really be far away from you."

I felt tears come up in my eyes and roll down my cheeks. Gabe put his arms around me. "Don't cry, Dru. This is but February. I don't go until autumn. There will be time enough for tears later." Waving and calling good-bye, he climbed up onto the cart and drove away. I stood watching as long as he was in sight, and I could not stop myself from crying.

I turned to go back to the house, but just then young Ann came running toward me. "Did you not see Reverend Parris come to our door?" She shouted when she was near me.

"No," I said.

"Mother told me I was to bring you with me at once to the Parrises'."

"Why?" I asked.

"The Reverend and his wife asked Mother to come and pray with them for the girls."

"Girls? Has some trouble befallen Abigail as well?"

"Yes, she has taken to flapping her arms like a bird's wings, and she goes about calling, 'swish, swish.' The Reverend's wife thinks it might do both girls good to see us."

Abigail? Why would she act that way? I said nothing.

"Why did Gabe Matson have his arms around you?" Ann demanded as we walked, and I was glad she was too excited to notice I had been crying.

I did not wish to discuss Gabe's news with her. "We are old friends," I said, "much like brother and sister. He was telling me good-bye, that's all."

Ann made a sort of huffing sound. "I believe Mother would think it unseemly, allowing a boy to embrace you that way. Besides," she said, "surely you have not forgotten that he is to be my husband. It would never do for you to be hugging my future husband."

I laughed. "I will keep that in mind should he actually become your husband. Until then, our embraces are really not your business." She made another sort of huffing sound, but I ignored her and walked quickly.

Tituba let us in the kitchen door. Her bright clothing had been exchanged for a plain gray dress, and her dark eyes seemed sad. "Come in," she said. "My master say I should give you supper with girls."

Betty and Abigail sat at the long kitchen table. It was a much different scene from the way that table had looked with a group of chattering girls around it. Betty stared off into space, and Abigail, elbows bent, kept lifting her arms as if trying to fly.

"Look," said Tituba, "friends come to see you. Betty, Abigail, you say hello now." Betty did not even turn her head in our direction. Abigail looked at us but for a second. She turned back then and continued to flap her arms.

"Where is my mother?" asked Ann.

Tituba motioned toward the great hall with her head. "They all praying in there. You take seat. Tituba make much good lamb pie for you all to eat."

I sat down on the bench with Betty, and Ann took the place on the other side next to Abigail. The meal was good, but I could take no joy in the food. Once I poked Betty hard in the ribs. "Oh," she cried out, but she did not turn her blank gaze toward me. I could not catch Abigail's eyes, and I became almost certain that she dissembled. What I did not know was why.

We ate in silence. When Tituba left the room at last, Abigail spoke in a quick whisper. "I don't know what is wrong with Betty. I think mayhap she has scared herself witless over what we were doing with Tituba and over what her father would do to us should he find out. My only defense is to join her condition. Otherwise they will come to the point of questioning me about what troubles her."

Just then Tituba came back into the room. Abigail got up from the bench, dropped to all fours, and began to crawl under the table. She made strange growling sounds as if she were an animal of some sort. I had to force myself not to laugh. Surely her aunt and uncle would be able to see through such antics. I imagined that Abigail would be getting a good whipping before the evening's end.

I was wrong. Tituba had carried food into the great hall, and as soon as the meal was over, the grown-ups came into the kitchen. Besides the minister, his wife, and Mistress Putnam, there were two others, Thomas Putnam's brother, Richard, and his wife, Hannah.

Betty and Abigail were moved to sit on small stools in the middle of the room. Ann and I stayed at the table. The grown-ups formed a circle around the girls, and the Reverend began to pray. "Our Father," he said, and immediately Betty put a hand over each ear. She began to shriek in a loud high voice. Abigail put her hands over her ears, too, and throwing herself off the stool, she began to writhe about as if in some terrible fit. The minister prayed more loudly, and the girls got louder, too. Sweat appeared on the minister's forehead even though the room was not warm. Finally, he stopped trying to pray and dropped his head in defeat.

"We must send for Dr. Grigg," said his wife.

"Yes," said Reverend Parris, "that is our only recourse." He sighed deeply and wiped at the sweat on his forehead with the arm of his jacket. "He is our only hope, but I do fear . . ." His words dropped off.

"You fear this is an ailment not of earthly origin," said Mistress Putnam. "I am right, am I not?" I looked closely at her face, and I was surprised to see what I could only interpret as glee in her eyes.

"Let us not speak of such a thing, dear lady," said Reverend Parris. "Not until we must do so."

On our walk home I announced. "Abigail is all pretense. Nothing ails her, not really."

Mistress Putnam did not respond. For one second, I thought she had not heard me, but then I realized she had chosen to ignore me. I could see she did not want to discuss Abigail's deception, but I could not let the subject go. "Mother," I said, "do you not see that Abigail is lying?"

"The child may exaggerate," she said, "but still that exaggeration could work for good. I will explain at another time."

The next day, we saw Dr. Grigg's buggy pull up in front of the Putnam home. Tituba's husband, John Indian, rode Mr. Parris's horse behind the buggy, and we knew the slave had been sent to fetch the doctor. Mistress Putnam waited for a bit, then took her cloak from its peg. "I must go over and see how the examination progresses," she said.

Ann and I hovered about the window, waiting for Mistress Putnam to return. She was gone a long time. When finally she came back, she did not speak until she had taken off her cloak and fixed herself a cup of hot tea. "I want you to go upstairs and sweep my chamber," she said to Rose, who frowned but left the room.

"What is it?" Ann said as soon as the door closed. "Tell us."

Mistress Putnam drew in a big breath. "Dr. Grigg says the girls do not suffer from an earthly illness." She stopped and looked to each of our faces. Her expression was quite serious, but I was fairly certain I could detect a bit of a smile playing about her lips.

"What is wrong with Betty, then?" asked Ann.

"Obviously, the girl is bewitched," said Mistress Putnam. "'Tis a terrible thing." She paused. "Yet, I can but hope some good may come of this. If this village must sound out witches, mayhap those who do our family harm will also be discovered."

I remember so clearly the cold shiver that went through my body when I heard her words. Oh, if only I had gotten up from that table and run out of that house as fast as my legs would carry me. I did not, however. I continued to sit beside the fire, making no attempt to save myself from the terrible fate that was about to befall me.

Chapter Twelve

Reverend Parris called in ministers from surrounding towns to come and pray for Betty and Abigail. Even the prominent Reverend Cotton Mather, who had taken in Boston's bewitched children and who had written a famous book about witches and witchcraft, came all the way from Boston. Our former minister, Reverend Deodat Lawson, came, as did Reverend Nicholas Noyes from Salem Town and Reverend Hale from Beverly.

We watched as the ministers came, some in buggies, some on horseback. "It is bound to stop now," said Thomas Putnam. "All that powerful praying will of a certain put an end to this bad business."

"I hope you are right, husband," Mistress Putnam said, but I could see by the look in her eye that she did not, in truth, want the end as of yet.

When the ministers were gone, the dreadful interrogation began at once. Over and over Betty and Abigail were questioned. Sometimes, Ann and I would be taken with Mistress Putnam to the Parris house. We would sit away from the circle of adults, some praying silently, that surrounded the girls. From the beginning Mistress Putnam's role was one of importance. Always either the Reverend or she asked the questions while the other adults remained quiet. The circle was confined to what Reverend Parris called "Our true friends. We must have only those who support us without question, those who we know do not bend their ears toward Satan."

The girls never responded to the question "Who has bewitched you?" Instead, Betty continued only to stare into space. Abigail was likely to make animal sounds. Once she broke from the group, ran to the great hall hearth, and began to climb into the fire. Her uncle, just in time, was able to catch the hem of her skirt and jerk her back.

It was unclear to me at first as to why Ann and I were so often taken to the Parris home. Later, of course, I understood far too well. It was on the second day when Betty uttered what seemed to be an answer to the question that had been asked her so many times.

"Who possesses you?" Mistress Putnam asked. Her eyes were aglow with excitement, and her cheeks were red. She leaned into the circle, and asked again, "Child, who has done this to you?" Just then a noise, as if from a dropped pan, came from the kitchen. "Is it Tituba?" Mistress Putnam said. "Does Tituba control you?"

"Tituba, oh Tituba," said Betty softly, and she began to cry.

"Tituba!" Reverend Parris shouted. "Do you mean Tituba has done this?" Betty only sobbed louder, but Abigail nodded her head. "In my own house! The woman has the nerve to do the devil's work in my own house!" He stormed from the room. I had seen the great leather strap that hung on a peg beside the cloaks and I knew that the Reverend had grabbed it because we heard him hit the table with it. Next he must have turned the strap on Tituba. We heard her cries of pain.

The minister's wife looked about the room, an expression of distress upon her face. "Perhaps it would be better for our guests to leave now," she said softly. "Go to your homes and pray. A great misery has befallen us."

On our way home, Mistress Putnam was much excited. "No doubt there are others," she said. "Tituba most surely does not work alone." She stopped walking and stood quietly in the snow for a moment. Then she reached out her arms to us. "I fear you two have been afflicted also because I know there are sinister people who would do us harm."

Ann's body began to twist. "I feel it, Mother," she said, "even now someone sticks pins into my body."

"And you, Drucilla, are you not tormented by our enemies?"

I opened my mouth to say I wasn't when a sort of odd sensation started in my toes and spread up into my body. Looking back, I know that I was surrendering to the power of suggestion. The emotion of the last few days had left me weak, and I began to believe myself touched by evil. "I . . . I think mayhap I am," I said, and I found myself starting to cry.

Mistress Putnam stepped away from us and lifted her arms toward the stars. "Ah, sweet children, I know you suffer, but remember God will not forsake you, nor will I, and I believe that at last we will learn who has murdered my children and kept us from obtaining the wealth and position rightfully ours." She dropped her arms then and began to walk quickly toward home.

At breakfast the next day, I could see that Mistress Putnam looked tired but still elated. Her words came tumbling out like a great gush of water. "I was with the Parris family most of the night," she declared as she passed our bowls to us. "Reverend Parris says he does not know what he would do without me. His wife is like Betty, not strong at all. She went on to bed while the Reverend and I prayed and questioned Tituba for most of the night. Tituba told us there are others in the town who worship Satan. At first she named no names, but finally she did indicate that Sarah Good and Sarah Osborne are guilty also. Abigail was awakened, and she admitted she had been pinched by specters of both women. At first she could not see their faces clearly, but when the names were given to her, she agreed." She pushed back the bright hair that had escaped her cap. "The three of them will be taken to prison today and brought before the magistrates soon to determine if they are to be tried."

Thomas Putnam set his bowl down hard on the table. "I don't know as I like this, your involvement in witch business."

"Don't be ridiculous, Thomas," she said quickly. "I *am* involved. Why, our own children have suffered, and so have you and I. We have been denied what is rightfully ours, and now we shall have it."

Thomas's face twisted with concern. "If some evil person has caused the death of our babies, of course, I'd want to know." He stood up. "It is just . . ." He shook his head. "I've work to do." I could see the concern still on his face as he left the room.

"What punishment will befall Tituba?" I asked.

"Tituba has confessed her sins," said Mistress Putnam, and her smile was big. "Her forgiveness is now in the hands of God. If she confesses at her trial, she will not be punished more."

We heard that afternoon that the witch hearing was to be held in a fortnight. Massachusetts had a new governor, Sir William Phips, and he had appointed a special court called Oyer and Terminer to handle the witch business. I learned later that the words meant to hear and determine. Mistress Putnam was disappointed. "I should think," she said when we heard the news, "that the governor would handle the trial himself, or at least that he and Lady Phips would be present for the trial."

On the day of the hearing all of Salem Village turned out. At first the proceedings were scheduled to take place at Ingersoll's

Ordinary, but it soon became apparent from the large group of people milling about that the tavern area of the inn was not big enough. The church would have to be used.

I dreaded the hearing, but clearly most did not share my feeling. Atmosphere at the meetinghouse reminded me of a fair. While we waited for the doors to open, children ran about the churchyard, some rolling hoops, others playing games of tag. Women stood in groups, their faces animated and their hands moving as they talked. Men gathered beneath trees to smoke pipes and talk quietly.

Mistress Putnam, who had been often with the Parris family, had informed us that Ann and I were to sit in front as part of the afflicted group. "Of course, I shall be there with you, in the first row. After all, I am Reverend Parris's right hand in all this."

When the doors were opened, Mistress Putnam, one arm holding to Ann and one holding to me, led us through the crowd. "Make way for the accusers," she said, and the pride was evident in her voice.

I was surprised to see Mary Walcott, Mary Warren, Susannah Sheldon, Elizabeth Hubbard, and Mercy Lewis already on the front seat. "Why are you here?" I whispered to Mary Warren when I was seated beside her.

"Oh," she said. "Have you not heard? We are all afflicted, just as Betty and Abigail are." She laughed. "I've been unable to work at all. My hateful mistress is in a terrible snit, but it cannot be helped. I am unable to work and must not miss these proceedings. The magistrate has said so."

They brought Sarah Good in first. As usual, she was dirty and her hair spilled wildly in all directions. I remembered how Mistress Putnam had said she was afraid of the woman. When I looked into her wild eyes, that same strange sensation began in my feet, the one I had felt before. An extremely nervous feeling grew inside me, and I began to shake. "She hurts me," cried out Abigail, and Ann let out an awful shriek.

There were two magistrates, John Hathorne and Jonathan Corwin. They had evidently decided between them that Hathorne would ask the questions. "Sarah Good, what evil spirit have you familiarity with?"

"None," said Sarah Good.

"Have you made no contract with the devil?"

"No."

"Why do you hurt these children?"

"I do not hurt them. I swear it."

The judge asked us to look upon Goodwife Good and see if she was the same person who tormented us. We did look at her. Abigail began to shake uncontrollably, so that Mistress Putnam changed places on the bench to hold her. "Yes," cried Ann, "she is one of our tormentors." I held out my hands in front of me. They felt as if they were being pricked by pins. We all nodded our agreement with Ann.

"What do you mutter when you leave houses after begging?" asked the judge.

"I say my commandments," said Sarah Good, "or a psalm."

"Repeat a psalm for us now," said Judge Hathorne. Sarah Good opened her mouth and muttered something, but her words could not be understood.

Judge Hathorne struck the table with his gavel. "Take her back to prison until her trial," he declared.

Next they brought in old Sarah Osborne, so weak that she had to be supported between two constables. I feared if I looked at the worn face, I would feel pity for her and be unable to testify against her. I had to remind myself that she was, after all, evil. Had I not often heard that from Mistress Putnam? Goody Osborne had been an outcast in Salem Village for as long as I could remember. When her husband had died, her hired man moved into the house with her, and later she had married him. Such behavior was indecent. I could see a real look of fear in Abigail's eyes, and my heart beat fast. Abigail had been acting earlier at the Putnam's, but now I believed she was truly frightened. Now Ann cried out that even at that moment she was being pinched by the old woman's specter.

"What contract have you made with the devil?" asked Judge Hathorne.

Goody Osborne shook her head. "None," she said, "I am more likely to be bewitched than to bewitch others." She then began a long tale about a dark-skinned man who dragged her by the neck about her house. Judge Hathorne, his elbow on the table, rested his head against his hand and closed his eyes. Judge Corwin, without even glancing up at the woman, continued to write something in his record book.

"She sent her specter to my chamber last night," said Ann, "and she did pull my hair most grievously."

At first I did not believe Ann, but then my mind rushed back to the night before. Had I heard Ann cry out while I slept? Yes, I believed I had. Just then a terrible pain shot through my head. "Her specter jerks at my hair even now!" I heard myself shout. Then the other girls, too, were holding their heads and screaming.

"Take her back to prison," said Judge Hathorne. "She is to be tried as a witch."

Next they brought in Tituba. She marched into the building, her head held high. It occurred to me that she might tell the real truth, might say that we had all been in league with the devil when we had begged her to tell our fortunes and to relate tales of witches. I glanced down the row, and saw looks of guilt on the faces of the other girls. There had been cries of pain when the first two women were brought in, but now we sat quietly and waited for Tituba to be examined.

Goodwife Good and Goody Osborne had, when questioned, spoken with short answers. Tituba, it seemed, had decided to enjoy herself. She waited for only one question. "Do you afflict these children?" asked Hathorne, and Tituba was off on her story.

"A tall black man come to me from Boston," she said in her best storyteller voice. "He bid me to write in his book. I tell him, I not know how to write, but he say if I take up his black book and wish my name written, it will appear. He tell me to hurt children." Here she shook her large head slowly several times, her eyes closed. Then she opened her eyes and continued to speak. "I tell him, no! I tell him I love these children, every one, and especially my little Betty. She be Tituba's special pet." She smiled sweetly down at Betty, who was crying soundlessly. "But the black man, he say I must hurt them. Goody Osborne and Goodwife Good, they come to me, too. They ride a great broom together, and they tell me I must hurt children. They grab my arms and twist them until I say stop. I will do it. I hurt children then, but I not enjoy doing it. I hate to hurt children, especially my little Betty." She began to sob then. "Tituba is so sorry for changing to a witch. Tituba hate witches and tall black men from Boston."

"Save that apology for your trial," said Hathorne. Then he looked down at the constable who had brought Tituba in. "Back to prison with her," he said.

I had not seen Gabe before the hearing, but he rose to walk beside me as I stood up and began to move to the door. "Dru," he said. "Why are you part of this?" I could see the angry turn of his mouth and the familiar way his brows were drawn.

"I did not choose to be afflicted," I said.

"This witch business is ridiculous. Those women are no more witches than you are."

"Did you not hear Tituba confess?"

He shook his head. "I heard a slave woman say what her master wanted to hear." He lowered his voice. "I find it hard to believe there are any witches, and I definitely don't believe we have seen any this day."

I stopped walking and reached for his arm. "Of course there are witches. Does the Bible not mention them?"

He frowned. "Some ministers say that the Bible did not mean what 'witch' has come to mean to us."

I dropped my gaze from his eyes. "You think I lied when I said my hair was pulled?"

"No," he put his hand over the one I had on his arm. "The mind does strange things, Dru. That's what Joseph Putnam says. People can get excited and believe things happen to them that don't, not really."

Suddenly I was angry, and I jerked my hand away from him. "You can tell your Joseph Putnam that Drucilla Overbey knows when her hair is pulled."

He looked at me for a moment, and I saw sadness mixed with anger in his face before he turned and walked away. I made my way outside where the sunshine on the snow almost blinded me. On the way home, Mistress Putnam walked ahead with her husband and the Reverend Parris, who had asked a church member with a buggy to drive his wife, Abigail, and Betty home. Ann and I were behind her parents. "Did it not feel grand?" she asked me in a quiet whisper. "There we were being looked at by everyone, us with all that power! It felt amazing,"

I stopped moving and grabbed her so that she stood still, too. "But you told the truth?" I asked. Suddenly it flashed through my mind to wonder when Tituba had changed from being our entertainer to being our tormentor, but I never let the question fully form in my mind. "I mean, it is true that Goody Osborne's specter really did come and pull your hair last night, is it not?"

Ann shook off my arm. "Of course my hair was pulled. Did you not feel your own hair yanked even as she stood before us?"

I stared down at my feet, then at the tracks I had made in the snow. "I did," I said slowly. "I think I did."

"Of course you did," said Ann, and she smiled. "Hurry, let us catch up with the others. I am starved."

That evening we all went to our bedchambers early. I fell asleep at once, but I was not allowed to sleep long. Someone shook me. "Wake up," said Mistress Putnam. "I must talk with someone."

I sat up and rubbed my eyes. "What is it?" I asked.

"Come," she said, "we can sit on the stairs. No one will hear us there." She stepped away from the bed, then looked back at me. "Bring a blanket," she said, "else we will freeze."

I took the extra quilt from the foot of our bed, wadded it in my arms, and followed her from the room. She walked down to the third step, sat down, and patted the spot beside her. "Here," she said, "sit beside me so that we can whisper."

I threw the quilt over my shoulders, sat beside her, and pulled the blanket to cover her, too. "I have had another vision," she said slowly. "This is the most important one I have ever had."

A feeling of dread came over me. Somehow I knew that I did not want to hear this, but I could not escape. "Tell me about it," I forced myself to say.

"It was most terrible." She put her hands up over her face. "I could see my dead babies. I saw, too, my dead sister and her lifeless babies." She shuddered. "So many dead babies." She put down her hands and gripped my hand hard between both of hers.

"Have you not seen them all before in visions?" I asked gently.

She nodded slowly. "I have," she said, "many times, but this time was different. This time I saw who had murdered them with her curses. I saw Rebecca Nurse!"

I felt my heart drop into my stomach. "Goody Nurse?" I shook my head. "No, there is some mistake. Goody Nurse is a church member. Her children revere her, and she is much loved by her grandchildren. Why, she has helped Gabe prepare for Harvard. She knows so much about the Bible."

She laughed. "Ah, yes, and the Bible says that devils believe and tremble."

"But, no," I said, "the woman is kind and loving."

"Not so loving when she and her husband all but stole that land they rent from the Allens just when Thomas and I had decided to buy it. We wanted to buy it outright, but, no, the Nurse family wanted it, and they got it." She let go of my hand, and I noticed she had made her hands into fists, which she held in front of her.

"Still . . ." I wanted to say something more to convince her she was wrong about Rebecca Nurse, but I knew the woman too well. When her mind was made up, nothing could be done to change it.

"Still, what?" she asked. "Oh, I know your friend Gabe will stand up for the woman, so will all her family and Joseph Putnam and all the Porters. That group always hangs together, just as they did to get rid of my sister's husband as minister, and just as they are dragging their feet about deeding Reverend Parris the parsonage as was promised." She stopped and drew in a deep breath. Then she put an arm around me and pushed my head down upon her shoulder. "You do believe me, don't you, Drucilla?" she said.

"Yes," I lied. "I believe you."

"Good," she said. "I want you to go with me tomorrow when

I accompany Thomas on his trip to Ingersoll's to swear out a complaint against the woman, and I want you to tell the judge that she has tormented you."

"But she has not," I said quickly. "Surely you do not want me to lie."

"When we know it will help convict such an evil woman, a little lie does not seem so bad." She shrugged her shoulders. "Who knows, she may yet begin to torment you even this very night."

I began to shake. "You are cold," she said. She stood up. "You must get back to your warm bed." She took my arm and pulled me up, then wrapped the quilt about my shoulders. "Good night, sweet daughter," she said.

For a long time, I lay in bed listening. When finally I was convinced that everyone in the house slept, I got up, found my clothing by the light of the full moon through the window, and dressed. I put on two pairs of stockings. It would be a long, cold trip to Mary Putnam's house. I carried my shoes with me so that my step on the stairs would be lighter. For fear of waking Rose, I did not dare go into the kitchen to get my cloak from the peg, so I carried with me the quilt from my bed. From the bottom of the stairs, I tiptoed across the floor of the great hall and let myself out the front door. Not until I was on the stoop did I put on my shoes.

Chapter Thirteen

The fates were good to me in that the night was not as bitter as I had expected. In fact as I hurried along, the quilt up over my head and shoulders, I felt no colder than I had sitting on the Putnams' stairs. It seemed to take forever to cross the fields and woods that separated the two Putnam houses. I recited riddles aloud to pass the time. "Little Nancy Etticoat, With a white petticoat, And a red nose: She has no feet or hands, The longer she stands, The shorter she grows." I smiled remembering the first time Gabe had asked me to solve the riddle. I hadn't been able to give him a solution, and he delighted in telling me that "candle" was the answer. Gabe thought he knew the answer about witches, too, but I was not so sure.

Finally the house was in sight. I stopped short and realized I had no plan. How did I think I would be able to speak to Gabe? Did I have to wake the whole household by pounding on the front door? I stared up at the windows on the second floor. I knew Gabe slept in one of those chambers, but I did not know which window was his. I walked around the house, looking upward. Still, I had no idea.

I picked up a small stone. Now I had to decide on which of the two windows on either side of the front door. I made my choice. Perhaps no one will respond by coming to the window. Perhaps I will wake Mary Putnam, but wouldn't she be awakened for sure if I pounded on the door? There was just as good a chance that I might hit Gabe's chamber and that he might come to the window. I pulled back my arm in preparation, then threw the stone with all my might at the window on the left.

It struck the house just beside the window. I held my breath. Right away the window was pushed open and a head appeared, Gabe's head. I dropped my quilt and waved wildly to him. He held up his hand to indicate I should wait, and then he was at the door and holding it open for me.

"Mistress Putnam is about to accuse Rebecca Nurse of witchcraft," I blurted out even before I was inside. Gabe led me into the kitchen. I stood beside the fire he stoked up and told him the whole story.

"I am going to wake Goody Putnam," he said. "You wait here." Soon he was back, and not far behind him was Mary Putnam, with a bed jacket over her nightgown.

"You don't believe that Rebecca is a witch," she said when I had told her the story. "Of course you don't or you wouldn't be here." She went to the kettle that hung over the kitchen fire, dipped water into a large mug, and made me a cup of tea. "You were right to come, and brave," she said as she handed me the mug. Then she turned to Gabe. "Go harness the cart. I want you to go to Joseph's house. He will know what to do. You can take Drucilla back on your way." Then she turned suddenly toward me. "Do you want to go back there? I will keep you here if you don't."

I could not look at Gabe as I spoke. "Yes, I want to go back, and I want to sneak in without their ever knowing I was gone. Ann Putnam has been kind to me and the little ones depend on me." I looked down at my feet, searching for words. "I couldn't just leave there, not now, anyway. I wish I could stay here, and I thank you for your offer, but I must return."

Gabe said nothing, only got his cloak and was out the door at once. "Sit down, child," said Mary Putnam when he was gone, "and drink your tea. It will warm you for your journey."

I sat down, but I could not stay. Rather I went to the window and watched for Gabe. When he drove the cart from the barn, I thanked Mary Putnam and ran out to climb up beside him. We spoke but little as we traveled. I listened to the sound of the wheels on the road and to the horse snort and whinny.

Just after we turned down the short lane that led to the Putnam house, Gabe spoke. "She is wicked, Drucilla. Surely you must know that."

"Not really," I said. "If you could but see how kind she is to me." I stopped to choke back a sob. "She is tormented inside and truly believes that torment to be the result of a curse. I know she's wrong about Goody Nurse, but she believes it. She really does."

"It is you who are cursed," he said, "cursed to be under her influence." He stopped the horse then and reached for my hand. "I fear this witch business will destroy you, Dru." He swallowed hard. "I could not endure losing you. Don't go back in there."

The touch of his hand on mine felt warm. "I can't just leave right now. You know how Thomas and Elizabeth depend on me. This will surely end soon."

"What will you do if Rebecca Nurse is tried? You won't testify against her, will you?"

"Oh, Gabe, I pray it won't come to a trial." I made myself pull my hand away from his. "I must go in." I climbed down quickly. I did not look back to see him drive away. I could not bear to watch his leaving. I had just time to climb the stairs, slip off my clothing and put my nightgown back on, when I heard Thomas

Putnam leave his bedchamber. He was always up before dawn, earlier than anyone else. I stepped out and followed him silently down the stairs. In the great hall, I cleared my throat, and he turned to look at me. "Drucilla, you're up early," he said.

"Please, may I speak with you?"

"What is it, girl?"

"I . . . I . . . Do you believe Goody Nurse is a witch?"

Thomas gave me a sad little smile. "I'm not a smart man, but Ann's a real thinker, she is."

I shook my head. "But you didn't answer. Do you believe Goody Nurse is a witch?"

Thomas frowned. "It's a fact that my Ann has suffered. We both know that, now, don't we? If she says it's Rebecca that caused it, well, then I'm obliged to stand by her. Isn't that right, girl?" He didn't wait for an answer, just turned toward the door.

I went back up the stairs. It would be a half hour or more before anyone else stirred. I got in bed to warm myself, and it was fortunate that I did so. After just a few minutes our door began to open, I closed my eyes and made my breathing regular. I heard Mistress Putnam step into the room. For the first time ever, I was afraid of her. Did she know I had been downstairs? Maybe she knew I had been away from my bed for a long time. I thought of the knife I had seen her hold on the first night I slept here. She remained by the door for a moment, then went out.

At breakfast, Mistress Putnam was cheerful and excited. "We shall go to see the magistrates this morning and your father will swear out a complaint against Goody Nurse," she announced cheerfully. Drucilla, Ann, would you like to go along with us?"

"Not I," I said too quickly. I put my hand to my forehead. "I have a dreadful headache this morning," I said more calmly.

"I'll go, Mother," said Ann. "Might we go into the Ordinary for a mug of cider? I have heard that John Indian frequently has fits of possession when he has a good audience and is likely to get a pence or two."

"John Indian is a fool. His ridiculous antics make us all look bad. No, we will only ask to see the magistrates. I want nothing to do with John Indian."

The Putnams' visit to the Ordinary did not take as long as I had hoped. I needed that quiet time. I played a game of draughts with little Thomas on the board Gabe had given him, and I tried not to think about what was about to happen to Goody Nurse.

Elizabeth came to lean against me as I sat on the floor before the fire playing with Thomas. "Please don't go off and leave us," she said.

I put my arm around her small body, the body I had washed, dressed, and watched over for three years. "Whatever gave you such a notion?" I asked.

"Mama said it. She told me you might not be here much longer." Tears filled her eyes.

"It's not true," said Thomas quickly. "Mama gets . . ." He paused looking for a word. "Mama gets all mixed up sometimes. Dru would never leave us. She loves us most dearly."

"I do love you both," I said, and I fought back the tears that wanted to come. I reached over the draught board to touch Thomas's cheek, and I hugged Elizabeth close. "It would make me very sad to leave you, but if ever I had to, you would always be in my heart."

"Dru would never leave us," Thomas repeated, and he jumped one of my men.

Mistress Putnam came home much excited. "Drucilla, you won't believe it!" she shouted when she opened the front door to the great hall. I was in the kitchen giving the young ones their noontide meal, but I heard her clearly and stiffened myself for her announcement. "The magistrates told me that a petition is being circulated attesting to Rebecca Nurse's good name," she said, bursting into the kitchen. "How could the Nurse bunch have known to start a petition? They say there are already more than thirty names."

"That is interesting," I said, and I continued to slice bread.

"I told them I cared not a whit if some petition listed a thousand names. I told them the woman is a witch, and I will see her brought to trial for the horrors she has visited upon my family."

"Let me get you some food," I said, but I knew she was too overwrought to think of eating.

"I'm hungry," said Ann, who had come in after her mother. "The magistrates were very kind to me. They asked me if I am still afflicted by the women in prison. I said not by them, but by Goody Nurse. Her specter came to my chamber last night and did hurt me most grievously. I battled with her most of the night."

I stared at Ann. Had she not been sleeping peacefully when I left to see Gabe, and when I returned? "When will Goody Nurse's hearing be?" I asked.

"On the morrow. The constable has already been sent to fetch her." Mistress Putnam paced up and down the kitchen. "Judge Hathorne says he is anxious to get the witch business settled so he can return to Boston." She stopped walking and smiled broadly. "I said nothing, but I do not think he will soon go home. There are more witches in Salem Village than he may suppose." She turned to me. "Drucilla, when you are finished with your meal, please come up to my bedchamber." Her voice dropped to a slow, sad sound. "The time has come for you and I to have a long talk."

I had just reached to fill my trencher with chicken pie, but I set the plate down empty. There was no way I could swallow food now. Yet, I did not hurry to leave the table. "Let me get you more, Thomas," I urged.

I glanced up to see Rose looking at me. The concern on her face touched me. "I'll see to the little ones," she said. "You might as well get it over with."

Young Ann laughed. "Guess what, Drucilla?" she said. "You may not be Mama's favorite anymore."

"Mind your tongue, Ann," said Thomas Putnam.

I slid from my place on the end of the bench and left the table. Everything went quiet in the kitchen as I left. I crossed through the great hall and started up the stairs. My steps sounded heavy in my ears. I knocked at her door, and she called for me to come in. Mistress Putnam lay stretched on her bed, a damp cloth covering her eyes. "Sit down, daughter," she said, "and pull the chair close. I've no strength left for speaking loudly. This witch business drains me, child, especially the latest episode." She was quiet then, and I felt she wanted me to say something.

I searched for something. "I am sorry you are unwell," I finally said.

She removed the cloth, and suddenly she was up, swinging her legs to the side to sit on the edge of the bed. "Are you?" She leaned toward me and peered into my face. "Are you really? I ask because I've begun to doubt that you love me at all."

I started to deny the accusation. "I—"

She held out her hand in a stopping motion. "No, don't speak. Now is a time for you to listen." She began to pace about the room. "I had a vision last night, Drucilla. It was a vision from God, or, should I say, a vision of God. He sat on a magnificent gold throne. There were two other thrones, one for me and one for dear Reverend Parris." She had moved to face the door, and I dearly hoped she might go out, but she only reached for the knob and pulled it closed. She whirled back to me. "While we sat there, God told me that I must not trust you. He said that you will betray me!" She reached for my arm and squeezed it hard. I could feel my entire body shaking with fear. "When the vision was over, I went to your bedchamber and discovered you were not there! Where did you go in the middle of the night, Drucilla?"

A calm came over me and I stopped shaking. "I went to see Gabe to warn him about Goody Nurse."

She sighed heavily. "Well, at least you know when not to lie."

"She is not a witch," I said softly. "She is a dear Christian lady."

Mistress Putnam drew back her hand, and I braced myself for being slapped. Suddenly, though, her mood seemed to change. Instead of slapping me, she touched my cheek. "My darling," she said. "Do you have visions of God?"

I shook my head. "I thought not," she said. "Then I wonder why you would think you know more about Rebecca Nurse than I do?" She let go of my arm and moved back to sit on her bed. "This Gabe is rather important to you. It will be painful for you when the friendship ends."

"It won't end," I said. "Gabe loves me and I love him."

She made a tsking sound. "He will no longer love you, I fear, not after you testify that Rebecca Nurse has tormented you."

I shook my head. "I won't do it," I said firmly. "I was caught up in the madness and frenzy at the other hearing. I truly believed those women were witches and that I was being afflicted. It won't happen at Goody Nurse's trial."

Mistress Putnam smiled. "What a pity. Then, of course, you will have the opportunity to testify at the trial of your precious Gabe."

"Gabe!" I jumped from my chair. "But you know Gabe has never harmed you. You know he is good and kind to your children."

"Sit down, child. I never said Gabe would be accused, not of a certain. I suppose it is rather up to you. Is it not?"

For a time I said nothing. Then I said, "I never thought you wicked. I always thought you truly believed those women to be witches. I thought you really were cursed by someone, but you know Gabe is innocent. For you to accuse him would be a mighty sin."

"No!" she shouted. "Occasionally the innocent must suffer so that God's cause can be advanced. Do you suppose all of those Egyptian soldiers who were drowned after the sea parted for Moses were wicked? I am sure they were not. Yet, they had to die so that God's perfect plan could be carried out. You will see. Once Reverend Parris and I have rid Salem Village of witches, you will see that the sacrifice of an innocent boy was worth it." She laughed then and reached out to pat my cheek again. "Of course, if you but cooperate at Rebecca's trial, your friend will be safe, at least for a while."

"I'd like to see him." I tried to keep all anger from my voice. "Might I go to see him now?"

She laughed, then lay back on the bed. "Do you think me stupid? You will not leave this house, not without me. I think you would forget us all, even Thomas and Elizabeth. You would run away. You may invite Gabriel for a visit here."

"He won't come to this house. Not now."

"Oh, I think he will if you word your invitation correctly. Rose will deliver your note." She yawned widely. "Run along, my darling. I am in need of a rest."

Relieved, I got quickly to my feet and headed for the door. "Drucilla," Mistress Putnam called. "You wound me. Have you no kiss for your exhausted mother?"

I turned back then, and without a word I kissed her cheek. It was a cold kiss, coldly given and coldly received. Downstairs I began to compose my note at once. "Gabe," I wrote. "I know you do not want to visit this house ever again, but I beg you for my sake to come just once more. I need to see you." I did not write that I wanted to tell him good-bye, good-bye forever.

Rose took the note. "Please stay until he has read it," I told her. "I would like to know his reply."

"What troubles ye?" said Rose. "Ye aren't acting right. What did the mistress say to ye?"

"Nothing. Nothing really. I am troubled over Rebecca," I said. "I don't believe she could be guilty."

She looked over her shoulder. "Be careful who ye say that to," she whispered. "We've got to be ever so careful."

While Rose was gone, I kept myself busy with Thomas and Elizabeth. "Come," I said to them. "Let's go up to the nursery."

"Will we do lessons?" asked Thomas.

"No." I tried to make my voice sound jolly. I reached for their hands and swung our joined hands between us. "This afternoon is for play only. Let's build a city with blocks."

"Yes," said Elizabeth, "and we can let our carved animals live there. Wouldn't that be fun, a town of animals?"

We were on the floor, blocks all about us, when Rose brought me the answer, "If you need me, I will be there this evening." Of course, I knew he would come. I knew, too, that it might well be the last evening we would ever spend together.

We had only just finished the evening meal, when Ann, who had positioned herself at the window to watch for him, called out with excitement, "It's Gabe! He is here."

I had my hands full of plates I had just gathered. Mistress Putnam reached out to touch one of my hands and whispered, "If you say a word about our conversation, I will know. If he makes trouble, I will move at once to have him arrested." She smiled sweetly. "If he should run, it will, of course, be you who goes to jail."

"I'll open the door for him," called Ann.

"No," said her mother, "let Drucilla do it. He is her beau. Don't interfere with their visit, but, Ann, you must stay with them. It would not be fitting for them to be alone."

As I walked to the door, I told myself to be calm and to smile. I had to act as if my heart did not race. "Gabe," I said when he stepped inside, "thank you for coming."

"You said you needed to see me, so of course I came." I could feel him studying my face. I could also feel Ann's presence directly behind me.

"I shouldn't have worded my note as I did." I smiled at him. "I felt lonely for you, that's all, and of course, I am concerned about Rebecca's trial."

"As are we all," he said softly, and I knew he was looking beyond me at Ann.

I had to change the subject. "Come sit by the fire," I said. "Doubtless you are frozen."

The older Putnams stayed in the kitchen during the entire visit. I knew Thomas was cleaning and polishing his guns. We could hear the low, steady sound of Ann Putnam reading her Bible. I longed to go into the room and snatch that holy book from her hands. It frightened me that she had truly convinced herself she was God's servant in Salem Village. I would have feared her less, I believe, if she realized she acted only from her own malice.

As soon as Gabe took his seat, young Thomas and Elizabeth were upon him. Thomas leaned against him, and Elizabeth climbed up to sit on his lap. "Sing to us, Dru. Please, please," said Elizabeth. "You have not sung for ever so long."

I was not at all sure I could sing without crying. "Do sing," said Gabe. He picked up Elizabeth and lowered her to the rug. "I've brought some good wood blocks for Thomas and me to carve." He pulled two small pieces of wood and a couple of knives from a leather bag he wore tied to his belt.

"I'll try," I said, "but my throat has been a bit scratchy of late." I started to move to get my lute, but Ann had already fetched it, and she held it out to me. I felt a moment of affection for the girl, affection and sorrow at what she had become, nothing more than a pawn for her sick, evil mother. I wondered in that instant what I would be like had Ann Putnam truly been my mother.

"Thank you, Ann," I said to her, and she smiled a real smile.

"'Greensleeves,' please," she said, and I began to pluck the strings and sing.

Alas, my love, you do me wrong
To cast me off discourteously
For I have loved you well and long,
Delighting in your company.

Gabe was busy with his wood, but every so often he would glance up at me and smile. I longed to memorize those smiles, the turn of his lips, the sweet, merry look in his eyes. I doubted if ever again I should be the recipient of those smiles, and my heart ached.

Gabe told us stories of the first Englishmen to come to Massachusetts and settle at Plymouth. "How big was the ship?" Thomas wanted to know, but my mind would not stay on the subject long enough to hear Gabe's answer.

Too soon the visit was over. Gabe stood. "I'll say good night now." He looked at me. It had been my habit to walk out with him.

Ann jumped up and was already at the door. "If Dru goes out with you, I am to go also. Mother says so." She was clearly delighted.

I ignored her as I got my cloak. Pretend she isn't here, I told myself. As we walked, we spoke only of the bright moon and the cold air. Just before Gabe climbed up on his cart, I said, "The Lord watch between me and thee, when we are absent one from the other." I tiptoed up and quickly kissed his cheek.

"I'll tell Mother," cried Ann, but neither of us acknowledged her.

"You're crying," Gabe said to me.

"About tomorrow," I murmured. Then, without waiting for him to climb up, I turned and hurried back to the house.

Chapter Fourteen

Somehow, I got through that night. The hearing was mid-afternoon. I had heard Mistress Putnam humming a song as she prepared herself to go. "You look pale, daughter," she said to me when I met her on the stairs. Doubtless you will feel better when that wicked woman has been put in her place."

The whole family went, even Rose, and Thomas Putnam took his largest carriage. He stayed in the back with the little ones and Rose, but I was marched to the front row with Ann and Mistress Putnam on either side of me.

The constable brought Goody Nurse in, holding onto her arm as if she might run away. She did not appear as weak as Goody Osborne had, but still it was plain that she was not a strong woman. She leaned heavily on a stick, but she did not duck her head.

I thought that Judge Hathorne looked distressed, and when he spoke to Goody Nurse, asking about the charges, his voice was gentler than when he had spoken to the others accused.

"I can say before my eternal Father that I am innocent, and God will clear my innocence," she said.

The testimony began. Mistress Putnam stood up and talked about how Goody Nurse had sent her specter to torment Ann.

"I have never afflicted no child, no, never in my life," said Rebecca Nurse, and her voice trembled.

Judge Hathorne leaned toward the woman. "Are you an innocent person relating to this witchcraft?"

Before she could answer, Abigail and Ann fell into convulsions, writhing and shaking on the floor, their eyes rolling back in their heads. Mary Warren and Mary Walcott began to screech and wave their arms. Susannah Sheldon grabbed at her neck as if to pry off unseen hands that choked her. Beside me, only Betty sat quietly. She stared ahead of her as if in a trance. Mistress Putnam poked me hard in the ribs with her elbow. "Speak out, Dru," she whispered, "Now!"

A great fear rose inside me, and I began to shake. "No, Goody Nurse," I said, but I knew my voice did not carry.

"Louder," Mistress Putnam said, "or I'll call out his name right now."

"Stop it!" I screamed. "Stop pulling my hair, Goody Nurse." I grabbed at my head.

Mistress Putnam stood and pointed a finger at Goody Nurse. "Did you not bring the black man with you to my home? Did you not bid me tempt God and die? How often do you eat and drink to your own damnation? I know you killed my babies with your curses." Her face burned with a redness that frightened me.

"Oh, Lord, help me!" cried Goody Nurse.

"You would do well if you are guilty to confess. Give God the glory." The magistrate's voice sounded pleading.

"Would you have me belie myself?" she asked.

Even after the constable had taken the woman away, I could not stop shaking. I sat quietly on the bench, blocking out the hubbub around me. I waited. I knew he would come, and I knew he would condemn me for what I had just done. I did not have to wait long.

Very soon Gabe was there. He stood in front of me, and he

looked at me with cold eyes. "You joined them." He spat the words at me. "You accused her by your actions, Drucilla. She will be found guilty at trial, and they will hang her. They will take away the blessed life of a saintly grandmother because of you and your friends." He did not pause for me to answer. It was just as well. What could I have said? He turned and walked away from me.

Mistress Putnam had stepped away, but she came to take my arm and help me to my feet. "Do not distress yourself overmuch concerning the boy. He is deluded now, but one day he will see."

I could say nothing. I felt weak and marveled that my legs held me up. They did hold me, and I got myself outside and into the Putnam carriage. Rose did not ride with us. She came over while we were loading. "I'll get myself back on my own," she said, and there was a scowl on her dark face.

Rose does not believe that Goody Nurse is a witch, I thought, and can let her feelings be known. I hunched low on the seat next to Ann, but I did not speak.

Rebecca Nurse was not tried at once. I am not sure why. Mayhap it was because the magistrates were busy holding hearings to determine who else among us should be tried for witchcraft. The number of girls who were afflicted grew and suspects were everywhere. Goody Curry, the midwife, was charged by Susannah Sheldon, and Mary Warren accused her mistress, Elizabeth Putnam. Sarah Cloyce and Mary Easty, sisters to Rebecca Nurse, were dragged from their homes, charged at a hearing, and thrown into jail. Even little Dorcas Good, four-year-old daughter of Sarah Good, was accused and imprisoned. The list went on and on.

I walked about as if in a dream. Nothing seemed real to me. When I had moments of quiet time, I thought about those first hearings. I had been so sure my hair was being pulled. Was the excitement so high that my mind was led to believe something was happening to me that wasn't? After Goody Nurse's hearing,

Mistress Putnam no longer demanded that I cry out accusations. But she did insist that I sit with the accusers. I watched the girls closely. Some, I knew, were simply lying, for one reason or another, but others I believe were caught up in a sort of group hysteria. I had to keep myself apart from them mentally to be certain I did not fall victim again to that group madness. I cannot explain—even as I write this in a place and time away from Salem Village—I cannot explain what had come over me early on in the witch hunt or what I saw later in others. One would cry out, and I honestly believe another would think she, too, suffered the same malady. What tricks did our minds play on us during those terrible sinister days in Salem? I only know that I will ever be on guard when I find myself caught up in a suggestion made by a group.

Mercy Lewis, a serving girl who lived with Richard Putnam, became a major accuser. She had testified against at least three people when she knocked on Thomas and Ann Putnams' kitchen door. "I am glad you answered," she told me. It was a bitter March day, but still she asked if I would go for a walk with her. "I want no one to hear what I say," she said. Mistress Putnam had gone to her bedchamber with a headache. Ann, who was usually watching me, was in some other part of the house. "Let us hurry out of sight else Ann will join us," I told her, and we hurried toward the woods.

"I want no more to do with accusations of witchcraft," she said when we were away from the house.

I was shocked. "Why?"

"Because it is lies, all lies." She pulled her cloak closer about her.

I stared at her, unable for a moment to speak, "But, Mercy," I finally said, "you fell on the floor. You screamed."

She closed her eyes. "Please, Drucilla, I think you know. It is why I came to you. I think you understand the excitement that comes over us. When I did those things, I believed. I always believe when I am in their presence." She opened her eyes. "It is as if a spell does come over me, but not a spell of witchcraft. Rather, it is a spell of excitement, a spell of being one of the group." She shrugged her shoulders. "I am never afflicted when alone. Are you?"

"No," I said. "Never. But others say they are."

"They lie. They lie for Ann Putnam and for Reverend Parris."

I could not deny that Mistress Putnam would ask her daughter Ann to lie. In truth she had asked me to do so, too. But Reverend Parris? "You believe a man of God would lie?"

She shrugged. "Betty Parris was afflicted in some way. Probably the child is as weak of mind as she is of body, and she was terrified by Tituba's stories. So do you not think it strange that the good minister and his wife have sent Betty away to live with relatives?"

"They did it for her protection," I said.

Mercy laughed a mirthless laugh. "Then why not protect Abigail, too?" She shook her head. "No, they sent Betty away because Abigail is so much the better liar. Surely you have noticed that many of the people who oppose Reverend Parris are among the accused."

Unable to meet her gaze, I kept my eyes down. "What do you plan to do, Mercy, and why do you come to me?"

"I came because I plan to tell the truth, and I hope you will stand with me."

I felt myself shaking my head from side to side. I could not tell her about the threat against Gabe. "I am not so sure as are you, nor am I so brave."

"Good-bye, then," she said, and she began to walk quickly away. I watched for a time, then turned back toward the house, hoping Mistress Putnam had been unaware of my visitor.

Providence was not with me. She waited for me in the kitchen near a window. "Was that Mercy Lewis?" She did not wait for an answer. "Why on earth did you not invite the poor girl inside? The wind is quite bitter. What did she want?"

I searched for a lie but could come up with nothing. "She is worried," I said finally. "She fears we may be mistaken in some of our accusations."

Mistress Putnam made a disgusted sound. "I am surprised not. My brother-in-law and his wife have often complained that Mercy is the dullest girl who has ever worked for them. The poor thing is not smart enough to understand the simple workings of a household. She can certainly not comprehend the hugeness of the battle we find ourselves waging against Satan."

"She means well," I said weakly.

"Never you mind about Mercy Lewis." She came to take my cloak from my shoulders and hang it on its peg. "I suspect things will work out for her just fine."

They did. Mercy went to the magistrates at Ingersoll's Ordinary the next day and told them that she had lied. She told them, or so we heard, that all of the accusations had been lies. I expected Mistress Putnam to be furious when she came home from the Parrises' with the news, but she was not. When she had told us the story, she merely smiled and shook her head. "That foolish, foolish girl," she said.

The next day Mistress Putnam went with Reverend Parris to see the magistrate. They took Ann and Abigail with them. Abigail came home with Ann and Mistress Putnam and they announced that Mercy was being arrested and taken to jail. A hearing would be held soon to determine if she, too, was a witch. "She did most grievously hurt me last night," said Abigail. "Her specter flew straight through the window glass of my chamber."

"She came to me also," said Ann, and she smiled. "She threatened me with a knife and wanted me to put my name in Satan's book, but I stood up to her. I told her she could kill me if it pleased her to do so, but I said I would never sign that evil book."

I could not speak. A great sickness began in my stomach. I had to run out the door and throw up around the corner. I stood leaning against the house when Mistress Putnam found me. "You are ill, daughter? Why? Does poor Mercy's troubles upset you so?"

"I do fear for her," I said softly.

"Don't fret, my darling. I'll wager a night in Salem prison will bring her to her senses." She came to me, put her arm around my shoulders, and led me back into the house.

Later that day, I was alone in the kitchen making a pie from dried apples. Rose had been given half a day off to visit her aunt. Ann came in to sit at the table where I worked. "Rose is a witch," she announced.

I had been rolling out pie crust, but I stopped and held the rolling pin in one hand. "You jest, I hope," I said.

Ann looked shocked. "You have never suspected her? I often have thought so, but now I am certain. Have you not noticed how often our porridge burns when she is away, just as it did this morning? Yet it never burns when she is here."

"Rose pays more attention to the porridge than anyone else. She knows she will be beaten should it burn." I went back to my pie crust.

"There are other things," said Ann. "Oftentimes I have discovered when I get up that one of my shoes is missing. I searched for a long time this morning. Finally, I gave up and came down here. There was my shoe, right beside the hearth."

"Misplaced shoes and burned porridge would hardly warrant an arrest for witchcraft," I said. "I think such a charge would give the magistrates a laugh."

"No." Ann frowned. "You should not make light of this. I think Rose sends her specter to torment me sometimes as I sleep." She rose and went to look out the window. "When Mother comes home from the Parrises' house, I intend to ask her to swear out a charge against Rose."

"You know women cannot make such a charge." I put my crust into a pan.

"She can tell Father to do it." She crossed her arms. "I am tired of the rude way Rose looks at me. She shows no esteem for me, none at all."

I told myself not to worry. Surely this nonsense would lead nowhere. Still, I stayed in the kitchen even after my pie was baked. I wanted to be in the room when Mistress Putnam came into the house.

When she came, she brought news that made Ann forget Rose for a time. "George Burroughs will be brought in for a hearing in a few days. Constables have been sent to Maine to bring him back for questioning."

"George Burroughs the minister?" I asked.

She nodded her head, her face full of satisfaction. "Several church members have sworn a complaint against him after I told what I know about him killing his wife."

"I did not know she had died," I said, and my mind was full of Peggy and the little ones of the household.

"Ah, yes, she has been dead now these several months. Reverend Parris thinks we may be on the verge of a great discovery. He says this man who passed himself off as a man of God may be the coven leader of our Salem witches. All of the evil may have begun with him."

"So Peggy and the other children have lost their mother and are about to lose their father." I made no attempt to disguise the sadness in my voice.

"Not necessarily." Mistress Putnam rolled her eyes. "Perhaps he will confess."

"Mama," said Ann, and I knew what she was about to say. "Mama, I want to charge Rose as a witch."

Mistress Putnam cocked her head and looked at her daughter. "Why, dear?"

Ann twisted her face with distress. "She pays me no respect, and at night she sends her specter to torment me."

"That is ridiculous, my dear," said her mother. "Rose cannot be a witch. The girl still owes us a year of service. Maybe next year."

Suddenly laughter bubbled up inside me. I put my hand over my mouth in an effort to hold it in, but the giggles broke forth and filled the kitchen. Mistress Putnam and Ann did not see the humor. I knew it was wrong of me to laugh when people might lose their lives, but still I could not stop myself. I left the kitchen and went up to my chamber. I wished I could tell Gabe about the conversation. Gabe would have laughed, too, but I would not be telling him. Gabe was no longer my friend. At the window I looked out to see the smoke from Mary Putnam's chimney.

To my surprise a familiar rider came into my view. It was almost as if my thinking of Gabe had made him appear, but he was not alone. A second man rode with him, and at first I did not recognize him. Gabe did not dismount, but the other man did. As he walked toward the house, his identity came to me. Joseph Putnam had come to call.

I ran out of my chamber and down the stairs, anxious to know the reason for this visit. I was in the great hall when the knock sounded on the front door, and I hurried to answer.

"Hello, Drucilla," Joseph said. "I've come to speak to my half brother's wife." I was uncertain as to whether I should invite him inside, but Mistress Putnam had come up behind me. I turned to look at her, and while I was doing so, Joseph Putnam stepped around me and entered the great hall.

"Well," said Mistress Putnam, "I was about to ask you to come inside, but I see you do not wait for invitations. Thomas is out in the field, but he should be in shortly. Won't you sit down and wait for him?" She motioned toward the settees.

Joseph shook his head. "I have not come to see Thomas," he said, "although I would have welcomed his hearing what I have come to say to his wife."

Mistress Putnam stepped close to Joseph. "And what is that, Joseph? What have you come to tell me?"

"Only this. You are a liar, madam, and I am here to tell you that if you touch any member of my household with your foul lies about witchcraft, you will be sorry despite all the magistrates and judges you might find."

He turned then and walked out the door. Without thinking, I went after him. I wanted to see Gabe, and I ran to where he sat on a horse. Suddenly, when I was close enough that I could have reached out to touch his leg, I realized what I had done by hurrying to see a person who wanted nothing to do with me. I stood very still, feeling my face grow hot. Gradually, I raised my eyes to see his face. Gabe looked down at me, his eyes cold. He looked at Joseph, who had mounted his horse. "Let's go," he said. They turned their horses and rode away.

Miserable, I walked slowly back to the house. Mistress Putnam stood in the doorway waiting for me. She put her arm around my shoulder and drew me inside. I wanted to push her arm away, wanted to tell her never to touch me again. However, fear for Gabe and myself kept me from doing so, and I followed her into the kitchen.

Chapter Fifteen

Mercy Lewis was released from prison. Mistress Putnam had visited Mercy and advised her to confess, told her to claim that she had been forced by other witches to make false accusations against the accusers. Shortly after that visit, Mercy was back beside us on the first row at the hearing for Reverend Burroughs. She was among the many who testified to the fact that the man had superhuman strength. Mistress Putnam said Reverend Burrough's specter had visited her and threatened to kill her just as he had killed his wife. When the girls on all sides of me began to cry out that they were being tormented, I felt my body starting to feel those odd sensations, but I quieted myself and remained silent.

When the hearing was over and we were back at the Putnam home, I claimed ill health and excused myself to go to my chamber. I was stretched upon the bed when Mistress Putnam came to talk to me. "Drucilla," she said, "I am concerned for you."

"I will be fine on the morrow," I said without looking up.

"You said absolutely nothing during the hearing." She came to stand beside the bed. "Do you doubt this man's guilt also?"

What could I say? I had seen what happened to Mercy Lewis when she dared to cross Mistress Putnam and her troop of afflicted girls. "I fear for his children. They have already lost their mother. If their father is hanged, what will become of them?"

She reached down to touch my shoulder. "Don't fret yourself over his children. Mayhap the man will consider them himself. He has only to confess his sins and turn in repentance to God. Some prison time may bring him to his senses. If he does not repent, his children are better off without him. Surely you can see the truth of that, daughter."

I nodded my head. Reverend Burroughs did not repent. Neither did Sarah Good, Sarah Osborne, or Rebecca Nurse. They were all tried on the same day. The petition with so many names testifying to Rebecca Nurse's good character did not help her in the end. The jury did actually find her innocent once, but the girls made such a fuss that the magistrate asked the jury to reconsider. That time Rebecca Nurse was declared guilty. The other trials were brief, and all three defendants were sentenced to death by hanging on Gallows Hill. The women would be first. Their execution was to be in a fortnight.

"Who knows," said Mistress Putnam at our evening meal. "They may all repent even yet." She smiled and shrugged her shoulders. "They will if they want to live. Look at it this way, children—if they repent we will all forgive them. If not, we will have an outing. It will be good for you all to attend the execution of those who do evil. Such events make a fine lesson for good Christian children." She began to eat her supper.

I would never have imagined that the next day would find me visiting Salem Town and Salem Prison. Mistress Putnam, I think, designed the trip so that I could see the horrors of the prison. She knew, I am sure, that I wished myself away from the accusers, and she wanted to show me what would happen to me if I stood against them.

"Have you ever been to Salem Town?" she asked me at breakfast.

"I have not," I told her.

She made a tsking sound with her tongue. "You have never seen the sea, then?"

I shook my head. "Well," she announced, "you shall see it this day." She cocked her head and studied me. "Yes, you have been wan and poorly now for a few days. I think it would do you good to breathe some good sea air. You and I shall ride with Thomas, who goes to Salem Town on business."

"May I go, Mother?" asked Ann.

"No, dear. You are needed here to see that Rose does her chores, and you must do yours, too, of course."

I would gladly have traded places with Ann, would have been willing to do chores all day and night rather than make the trip, but I knew better than to say so.

Salem Town was a long buggy trip from Salem Village. We left immediately after breakfast. I was allowed to sit behind Mistress Putnam and her husband on a bench all to myself. I did enjoy the journey. Blocking out the conversation between the Putnams, I looked at the fields and homes along the road. I imagined that I was having a conversation with Gabe about what I saw. For a time our route followed the river. Long before we came to the point where the river joined the sea, I could smell it. When at last I saw that great ocean, I forgot for just a brief moment about all of my misery. Two large vessels were moored near the shore. I could see their decks and the men working there. The sight gave me some measure of hope. If ever I should be able to get myself free from the woman who sat in front of me, I would travel on a ship. I would go to sea! When we reached the town, the buggy turned down a street and I lost sight of the sea.

After a few more turns, though, the ocean was visible again, but so was the prison. It sat at the end of a street with no houses or shops in sight, a long, low building made mostly of stone. It was built very near the water, and I could see that small openings among the stones must have been made to let seawater in when the tide was really high.

"Here we are, daughter," Mistress Putnam said in the same tone that she might say we had arrived at a neighbor's home. "I want you to go inside with me, my dear, and we will take this to the women there." She reached to lift a good-sized basket from beneath the front seat.

Thomas Putnam stepped down and helped his wife to alight. While he reached for the basket, I jumped down. He handed the basket to me. I spread back the cloth cover. Inside were several loaves of bread. Mistress Putnam led me into the building, where she spoke with a jailer, a large, slow-moving man. She told him who she was, and he recognized her name at once. She explained that we had come on a mission of mercy, and that we hoped some of the women would be touched by our kindness and confess.

"Visitors are not usually allowed except one per prisoner when they first come in," he said, and, hesitating, he looked at her closely. He scratched his head and said, "I suspect the magistrates would say you are an exception."

Mistress Putnam smiled. "Actually, I am not well today, so I will send my daughter, Drucilla." She turned to me. "Follow this good man," she told me.

When his back was turned, she whispered to me, "I need not go in. This lesson is for you, my dear."

I hesitated, and she gave me a slight push. Knowing I could not defy her, I swallowed hard and walked behind the jailer. He opened a heavy door and motioned for me to enter. Coming from the light into the darkness made it impossible for me to see. The foulest odor imaginable filled my nostrils and forced me to raise my arm and cover my nose with my sleeve.

I took one step into the room, and the heavy door closed behind me, leaving me in a dark dungeon. When my eyes had adjusted some, I saw women on the floor, their legs in heavy chains. Tituba was there, and all the others. Sarah Osborne lay in a heap against one wall. Not far from her, Sarah Good and little Dorcas huddled together. I had heard that special chains had to be forged for Dorcas's tiny legs. Still, it was a shock to see the child fastened that way.

Rebecca Nurse and her two sisters, Mary Easty and Sarah Cloyce, sat together in the corner. I saw Elizabeth Proctor and many others. I broke the bread into big chunks and handed it out. I bent to shake Goody Osborne's shoulder, but I could not rouse her. "Let her sleep, child," said Rebecca Nurse from across the room. "She is dying, and that is a blessing for her. They won't get to cheer while she swings."

I went to the three women, glad the light was too dim to see their faces clearly. I did not want to see the pain and exhaustion that I knew must be there. I also did not want Goody Nurse to recognize me, but she did. "You're Drucilla," she said, "Gabe's friend."

"Yes," I murmured, and my heart ached with the knowledge that I should have answered no to the part about being Gabe's friend. I braced myself to be yelled at, but they did not condemn me as I had them.

"How did you get in here?" asked Rebecca's sister Sarah. "Visitors are not usually allowed."

"Do you still live with Thomas and Ann Putnam?" Rebecca asked.

I did not want to say yes, but for some reason I could not lie. "I do," I said after a moment.

"That is why they let her in," Rebecca said to her sisters. She reached a shaking hand out as if to touch me. "Ann Putnam is a dangerous woman. Be careful of her. She could turn on you at any time."

"I know," I said with misery, as I backed toward the door. "I should go," I said.

Mary Easty, Rebecca's other sister, held out her hand to me. "Wait, please," she said. She put her hand into her pocket and brought out a piece of paper. "I have written to the magistrates," she said. "If I give it to you, would you see that they get it?"

"I . . ."

"Please, child. See that it doesn't fall into Ann Putnam's hands." She held the letter out in my direction.

"I will find a way," I said, and I took the paper and put it in my pocket. I pounded on the door and slipped quickly through when it opened. Saying nothing to the jailer, I hurried outside and leaned against the wall. My knees felt weak, and I had trouble breathing for a moment. When I was somewhat recovered, I looked about for Mistress Putnam, but I saw nothing move save a group of seagulls. Could it be that she had left me? It would be the best thing that could happen to me. I could find some sort of work. Even living in the streets would be better. I heard the sound of horses then and carriage wheels. She was back in the carriage with her husband and coming toward me. Had he completed his business so quickly? I sighed. There may have been no business at all. The entire purpose of the trip may have been to show me what happens to those accused of witchcraft.

"Did you hand out the bread to the poor wretches?" Mistress Putnam asked when the carriage stopped beside me. I nodded and she bent down to take the basket. "Did anyone confess to you?"

"No," I said, and I climbed up onto the second seat.

"Well, there will be many more in prison before this is over," said Mistress Putnam.

She was, of course, right. They were marched through the meetinghouse one after the other like lambs to the slaughter. Some few saved themselves by confessing, but most stood firm in their denial of witchcraft. Every day there was at least one hearing and one trial. Spring had come to the village, but farmers attended the witch proceedings and let their fields go unplowed. It was as if the entire village had gone mad.

I gave Rose Mary Easty's letter to the magistrates, and she delivered it when she was sent on an errand to the village store. Mary had begun her long letter with "I petition your Honours, not for my own life, for I know I must die, and my appointed time is set, but . . . that no more Innocent Blood be shed." Her plea did no good.

The madness spread to neighboring towns, too. The afflicted girls, with Abigail Williams and young Ann Putnam always among the group, were frequently taken to other villages to search the faces of people completely unknown to them so that they could cry out the witches there.

One old man named Giles Cory refused to make a plea of either innocent or guilty because he knew the law did not permit a trial until a plea had been made. He was put in a field with a large board covering his chest. He was asked again to make a plea and when he refused, a big rock was placed on the board. Over and over the process was repeated. When the question was asked, Giles Cory would only reply, "More weight." Finally, of course, his life was pressed from him.

I was fortunate enough not to be forced to witness Goodman Corey's crushing, but Mistress Putnam was there, and she spoke of it later with obvious pleasure. "These people think they can win, but they will soon learn. Justice will be done." She smiled broadly.

We were at supper in the kitchen. I had to force myself to partake of the stew. Each bite made me want to retch. Had I not eaten Mistress Putnam would have fussed over whether or not I was ill, all the time making thinly veiled threats about what happened to people who turned their back on righteousness. "Those who are not for us are against us," she would say, and her blue eyes would burn holes in me.

I was not allowed to miss Rebecca Nurse's hanging. She was hanged along with Sarah Good. Sarah Osborne, true to Goody Nurse's prediction, had died in prison. The event was scheduled for a morning. "We will pack a noontide meal," said Mistress Putnam. "That way we can eat after it is over and be back at the church for John Proctor's trial in the afternoon. We will make a holiday of it." She scurried about the kitchen putting bread and cold chicken into a big basket. At the scene, she insisted we all get down from the wagon and sit on a blanket to eat.

I had not thought to see Gabe on Gallows Hill, but he was there with Goody Nurse's son Samuel and Joseph Putnam, all three standing as close to Rebecca as the constable would allow. How many weeks had it been since I last saw Gabe? I could not be sure. Life for me now was one big blur. I thought my old friend seemed taller, and all roundness, all sign of boyishness was gone from his face. Gabe Matson had become a man.

Samuel pushed passed the guard just before his mother was blindfolded. He kissed her worn cheek and whispered something in her ear. She stood straight and proud while her eyes were covered. The hangman threw her over his shoulder and climbed the ladder. I turned my head before he reached the top. There had been cheers from the crowd when Sarah Good swung, but no one made a sound when Rebecca Nurse was pushed from the hangman's shoulder. The sun went behind a cloud at just that moment. Avoiding the swinging body, I looked around at the people. They stood about in hushed groups, and I believed at that moment many of the people had a moment of sanity, when they wondered how their village had come to this terrible day.

The moment of silence passed, and people were stirring about, talking to others before they left. Mistress Putnam was engaged in a conversation with Reverend Parris and a man I did not know. Thomas Putnam stood near the carriage. "I am sorry, girl," he said to me. A moment of anger shot through me. How could he do whatever she wanted him to? Then I looked into his simple, sad, and confused face. I could not blame Thomas Putnam.

I turned to climb back up to the carriage seat, but young Ann pulled at my dress. "Let's go over to speak to Gabe," she said. "He never comes to see us these days."

"He doesn't come because he wants nothing to do with any of us," I said.

"Mayhap he wants nothing to do with you, but I think he will talk to me." She turned away from me and walked toward where Gabe was getting on his horse.

Ann reached him just as he settled onto the horse. I could tell by the way she looked up at him that she was saying something, but I could not hear what she said. I saw his mouth move briefly and then he was gone.

She came back to the carriage, a sullen look on her face. "Would he talk to you?" I asked.

She tossed her head. "Said he had no desire to speak to any afflicted girl." She leaned around me to stare off in the direction where he had ridden. "I'll think of a way to make him change his mind. I may need to tell him that he and I are to be married. He has no business letting these witch trials keep us apart."

An enormous fear began to grow in the pit of my stomach. "Don't tell him anything about your vision," I said, but I knew she would do whatsome ever she pleased. I knew, too, with a terrible certainty, that I had not seen the worst of the witch business. Not yet.

Although I never looked directly at them, I could see from the corner of my eye that the bodies were still hanging when we drove away. I leaned from my seat to speak to Mistress Putnam. "When will they be buried?" I asked.

"They won't be buried, well, not as we think of it, anyway. No witch could be laid to rest in a Christian burial spot. The constable will dispose of the body in some other manner. You should not fret yourself over such matters. We need to turn our thoughts to finding those witches still hidden in our community."

I did fret myself, though, over where Rebecca Nurse would rest. Others did also. A few days later Rose told me that Samuel Nurse had taken a small boat the night of the hanging and rowed down the Crane River to the North River and stopped at a spot near Gallows Hill. He had found his mother's body in a ditch, partially covered with dirt and had taken her home to be buried secretly on the family property.

"Ye aren't so sure about this witch business anymore are ye?" Rose asked after telling me the story. We were in the field planting flax. Tears gushed from my eyes, and I laid down my bag of seed so that I could dry my eyes.

"No," I said, when I could speak. "Not so sure at all."

"Ye best be careful," she said, and she used her hoe to cover seed. "I am safe at least for another year, but there is nothing to stop them from turning on ye." She looked at me and smiled. "I knew ye was too good to be a real part of this family. They are most truly wicked."

Chapter Sixteen

Gabe had long since stopped coming to meeting to hear Reverend Parris preach, so I was most surprised to see him there on the following Sunday for the second sermon. I sucked in my breath in astonishment when he came through the door just before service started. He told me later that he came only to see my face, that he knew we could never be friends again, but that he grew lonely just for a glimpse of me. I was touched, of course, by his desire to see me, but it pains me so to know that I was the reason for his coming that morning, that I was the reason, then, for what befell him.

He stood at the back of the church just as young Ann, little Thomas, Elizabeth, and I did, but we were separated from Gabe by several other young people, he being near the door. From time to time during the sermon, I would fancy that I felt Gabe's eyes on me, but when I glanced at him, he did not seem to be looking in my direction. I ached to slip through the others and stand beside him. Of course, I did not.

When the sermon was over, I did hurry out. He stood just in front of the church, and I made my way around a group of children to get to him. I had made up my mind to tell him simply that I had missed him. I never got that chance. Young Ann had hurried even more than I had. She had already reached Gabe, and as I approached them I heard her say, "You and I are to be married. I have seen it in a vision. So you need not waste time being angry at me over the trials. In the end those silly hangings won't matter to you at all."

My heart sank. Oh, if only I could have stopped her from making that foolish speech. I saw Gabe's face grow red with anger. For a moment, I thought he might say nothing, but he did. "You call the hanging of one of the most saintly women in this entire commonwealth silly." He leaned toward Ann. "Girl, will you get this straight. I would rather be hanged myself than have anything to do with you and your despicable family. Your vision of our marriage is as false as your vision of witches. I would to God that I might never see your face again." He whirled away from her then, went to where his horse was tethered, threw himself upon the animal, and was gone. I stood beside Ann, and we both watched his departure in silence. Ann's face was a picture of hatred.

Saying nothing to Ann, I went back into the church to collect Elizabeth and young Thomas. I was encouraged because as the family walked home Ann made no comment about Gabe. Mistress Putnam walked ahead of us with little Thomas and Elizabeth. They were excited by actually having their mother's attention, and they chattered all the way about their plans for the evening when there would be no chores. I could still see anger in the set of Ann's mouth and in her eyes. I prayed as I walked that she would forget Gabe's words. I also searched my mind for something I might say to her, something that might soften her heart toward him. When the Putnam house came into sight, I felt new despair because I had been able to come up with nothing to say to her.

Through the evening meal, I all but held my breath, waiting.

When we had finished eating and the kitchen had been tidied, I did not sit beside the fire with the others. Instead, saying I was unusually tired, I went directly up to the chamber I shared with Ann, glad to have some time to myself for more thinking.

My time was brief. Hardly had I put on my night clothes and got into the bed when Ann appeared. I had blown out our candle, but she carried a new one with her. It illuminated her face, and seeing that familiar expression of anger made me shudder. I closed my eyes quickly and hoped she would think me asleep and say nothing. She may have caught a glimpse of my open eyes, or, and more likely she cared not that she disturbed me. "Drucilla," she said petulantly, "you may as well sit up. We are going to talk, whether you want to or not."

I stopped myself before screaming at her. I had to be calm, had to try to sooth her feelings. To gain time, I rubbed at my eyes, hoping she would believe I had truly been sleeping. I would act as if I did not know what she wished to discuss. "What?" I said. "Has something happened downstairs?" I raised myself, and she sat down hard on her side of the bed, making our faces close to each other.

"Don't try your deception with me." She all but spat the words at me. "You know perfectly well what has happened. Did you not hear the hateful words Gabe Matson spoke to me? Surely you must know I will not let him get away with speaking so to me."

"Ann," I said gently, and I reached out to touch her arm. "Please, I beg you. For my sake, please do not cause Gabe pain." I sighed. "He does not understand what is happening, and he has been greatly distressed by the hangings. Rebecca Nurse was dear to him." I thought quickly that I must not praise the woman. "He did not see the true person. You cannot fault him for caring for her when she showed him only kindness. He is deluded, that's all. Give him time. He will come to see the truth of the great battle we fight with Satan."

I studied her face, and saw her expression soften slightly. "You think he will change his mind about me?"

"I do." I lied with no hesitation. "Just be patient."

Even as I uttered that last phrase, I thought about how patience was not a Putnam trait. I closed my eyes and rolled over, my face in my pillow. Had I convinced Ann to take no action against Gabe? My heart beat so loudly I wondered that Ann did not hear and ask me about the noise. I knew exactly what happened to those this family thought of as enemies. I feared for Gabe so much more profoundly than I had ever feared for him before. Should I try to contact him? Mayhap I could warn him. I knew he would refuse to make any pretense of being friendly with young Ann. Would he consider leaving the area? There was nothing to hold him in Salem Village, nothing except me. I let my fancy roam wild, imagining Gabe and I driving away together, leaving all the ugliness behind us.

I yanked my mind back to reality. I would go this very night to warn him. I would not throw the rock at his window as I had on that other trip. If he were to look down and see me, he might not come to the door at all. This time I would knock loudly on the door. Mary Putnam should know about Gabe's danger. Surely she could persuade him to leave the village early. He would go soon to college, anyway.

It seemed to be a long time before Ann's breathing became the rhythmic sound made by a sleeper. I slipped out of bed and dressed in the dark. Just before I moved to the door, I decided to take with me the only possession I truly valued. I wanted to be ready should Gabe actually ask me to go with him away from Salem Village. I went to the bureau drawer, opened it quietly, and felt about until my hand closed over the miniature of my mother. I also took the plaque Gabe had given me, and Thomas's star. I tied the three objects together in my nightgown. I tiptoed out the door.

The house was in total darkness. Just outside the door to my chamber, I stood listening. No sound came to my ear save the ticking of the big clock in the great hall below. Carefully, I made my way down the stairs and into the kitchen where I took my cloak from the peg. Rose lay sleeping on her mat before the hearth. Not wishing to wake her, I stepped back into the great hall where the door would open with less noise than the one in the kitchen.

Looking over my shoulder to make sure no one was watching, I moved out into the darkness and bumped at once into Thomas Putnam. "Whoa, girl," he said, "where on earth are you going?"

My mind raced. I thought to run until I realized his hands gripped my upper arms. "For a walk," I murmured. "I couldn't sleep."

Stepping backward, I was pressed back across the threshold. It was then that I heard Ann's voice. "She was going to Mary Putnam's," she shouted from the dark stairs. "She wanted to warn Gabe Matson that I might have him charged as a witch."

"You best wake your mother," said Thomas, and I heard Ann's feet running back up. Neither Mistress Putnam or Ann came down immediately, and I knew that they must be talking. Thomas held to my arm until I was seated on a settee. He poked up the fire and added two more logs. "I wish this hadn't happened," he said, and I knew he meant it.

When they came down the stairs, Mistress Putnam sat beside me. Thomas and Ann sat across from us on the other settee. "Ann has just told me some rather distressing news. She says Gabe took liberties by kissing her. When she rebuffed him, she began to suffer terrible pain on her lips."

I buried my face in my hands.

"That's right," said Ann, and just now his specter floated into my window and pulled off my nightgown."

"Daughter," said Thomas, "why did you not tell us this earlier?"

"I told Drucilla," she said, "and she begged me not to tell either of you. Now she has betrayed us by trying to warn the monster."

Mistress Putnam pulled my hands away from my face. "Look at me, Drucilla," she demanded. "Is this all true?"

"No." I made no attempt to hide my anger. "He did not try to kiss her. She told him about her vision of being married to him, and he said he would never marry her or anyone else who lived here. I feared she would cry him out as a witch, and I wanted to warn him to go away from Salem Village."

Mistress Putnam put one hand over my right hand, held in a tight fist in my lap. "Tsk-tsk," she made the sad sound with her tongue. "This makes me so sad to know that the boy has fallen away to the devil, and it makes me even sadder to know you, who has been treated as our own daughter, would seek to warn a witch."

Knowing denials were useless, I said nothing, as I held on with my left hand to the arm of the settee and wished myself away from that house. Mistress Putnam turned her gaze toward her husband. "Well, Thomas," she said, "we've nothing for it but to swear out yet another complaint." She shook her head slowly. "What has life in Salem Village come to? Where will it all end?" I had thought to remain silent. Yet, a great moan escaped me, and I wished myself dead.

Mistress Putnam led me back up the stairs, and after Ann and I were both inside our chamber, I heard a pounding outside the door. "Father is nailing the door shut," said Ann with a toss of her head. All hope was gone from me. Somehow I got my clothing off, untied the treasures I had wrapped in my night gown, and put it on. I pulled the covers over my head and hoped I would be allowed to stay there.

For a time it seemed I might indeed be left alone. I heard Ann moving about the next morning while she dressed, but I kept my head covered. Evidently Thomas Putnam had made a board to serve as a sort of bolt across the door because I heard wood sliding after Ann had pounded on the door to be let out. When Ann was gone, I got up and went to the window. There was the smoke from Mary Putnam's fire, just as it had always been. I did not want to imagine Gabe being led away in chains, but I could not keep the picture from forming in my mind.

There was nothing in my chamber to help me pass the time, and naturally the situation made me think of prison. At least I had light from the window, and I would not be cold or wet from seawater. My legs were not in chains. It came to me that I might as well remain in my nightgown, but I decided to get dressed, anyway. I was putting on my petticoat when, suddenly, though, a thought flashed into my mind and a bit of a plan began to grow.

It was evening when the wooden bolt slid next. Rose stepped into the room. "I've been sent to fetch ye," she said. "The mistress fears ye are hungry and lonely," she said when the door closed behind her. "They want ye to come downstairs now. She says she is certain ye will be glad to be part of the family again." She laughed. "Me, I'd sooner be part of a wolf pack."

She turned and went back through the open door. When I made no motion to follow, she stepped back into the chamber.

"Make it easy on ye self," she said. "If ye stay here, they will but come and drag ye."

I knew she was right. Besides my plan made it necessary for me to cooperate with them. Suddenly, though, I wanted desperately to tell someone. I reached for her hand, pulled her back into the room, and closed the door. "I am going to pretend to be reconciled to their plans," I said, "but I want you to know I'm not." I bit at my lip. "I have an idea, mayhap a way to stop this madness."

She smiled at me, and I realized I had no memory of ever having seen her smile. "May providence shine on ye," she said.

We left the chamber then. My heart raced as we went down the stairs, but I kept pulling in deep breaths of air and forcing myself to remain calm. I cautioned myself against rushing. If I appeared too eager, the Putnams might doubt me. I must make myself seem to come gradually to their way of thinking.

I followed Rose into the kitchen where the family sat around the long table preparing for supper. I did not meet anyone's eyes, rather studied my shoes. "Well, Drucilla," said Mistress Putnam in a pleasant tone, "have you learned your lesson?"

Still not looking up, I said, "I am most regretful to have grieved you, Mother," I said. "Still I cannot say that my heart does not sorrow for my old friend Gabe. I know he is not in league with the devil."

"His hearing will be held on the morrow. I will spare you from attending, but I am afraid his guilt will certainly be established. In fact, there is something I should have told you earlier." She rose, came to me, took my hand, and led me to a place at the table. "I hate to say this, but I have known about Gabe Matson for some time." She sighed deeply. "I detected a look about his eyes, a look of deception. I have never really trusted him, albeit he did seem pleasant."

I took my place at the table and was surprised to find myself truly hungry and eating the deer meat stew most eagerly. I waited until my bowl was almost empty before saying, "What would you say should I ask to attend the hearing? Mayhap it would help me settle his guilt in my mind."

Mistress Putnam looked at me for a long time before she spoke. "For some time, daughter, I have felt a pulling away on your part. I have believed you wished yourself away from us."

A great surge of excitement came to me. This was my chance. "Oh," I said, "I want you to believe that I am of a certain with you. I want you to trust me and deem me your greatest supporter." My voice, I knew, sounded sincere because each of my well chosen words was completely true. I desperately wanted her trust.

She studied me for another long moment. Finally she said, "You shall go, and you shall sit beside me in the front row."

"Thank you," I said, and I went back to my stew.

Sleep did not come to me at all that long night. Rain fell hard against the roof. I lay quietly beside Ann, thinking of Gabe in the cold, wet prison, and I spent much time in prayer. The next day, I moved as if in a dream. Somehow I got through breakfast. When I found myself in the carriage and headed toward the church, I began to shake uncontrollably.

"Mama," Ann called from beside me. "I think Drucilla is about to have a fit."

"I am shaking." I said. "This is most painful for me." My voice broke and tears gusted from my eyes.

Mistress Putnam, on the seat in front of us with her husband and little Thomas, turned and strained to reach my cheek with her fingertips. "I will be beside you, daughter," she said. I willed myself to stop crying and dried my eyes on my dress sleeve.

At the church, I kept my eyes down. People milled about on the grounds, but we went straight in with Mistress Putnam leading Ann and me to the front row. Other girls were there already: Abigail Williams, Susannah Sheldon, Mary Warren, and on the end was Mercy Lewis, the girl who had tried to escape being among the afflicted. I looked directly into her eyes. How did she feel about this business after being in Salem prison? I wondered if she might help me, but her face showed no emotion, told me nothing.

The plan I had made was that I would not look at Gabe's face. Being not at all sure I could look on his countenance and go ahead with what I had to do, I thought to look always just slightly over his head. When the proceeding began, they brought him in, one constable walked before him and one after. I forgot my intentions and looked at him. His hands were tied behind his back. A huge greenish blue bruise covered one side of his face, and it hurt me to know someone had struck him a mighty blow. Still, his shoulders were not bent, and he held his head high.

The magistrate read the complaint Thomas Putnam had sworn out against Gabe. The last word had barely been uttered when young Ann screamed out, "Stop him! Someone must stop him!" She held her arms up as if to protect her face. "His specter even now tries to put his hands on my cheek."

I looked at the dear face that was my first memory. How I loved those clear blue eyes, and, oh, how I hated to do what I knew I must. "He came into our very chamber last night and did say despicable things to us!" I screamed. Before I looked away, I saw his expression. He looked as if the life had been knocked from his body.

"I was in chains last night, sir," said Gabe.

"His specter!" shouted Ann, and Mary Warren fell to the floor, her eyes rolled back into her head. Susannah Sheldon began to shriek and use her hands to slap at something unseen about the bodice of her dress.

"Take him back to prison to wait for his trial," said the magistrate. I watched him stand, and I saw the constable shove him down from the platform. When he fell, I jumped, without thinking, to my feet, but then I remembered, and forced myself down. Four other people were brought in for hearings that morning, three women and a man. I watched the other girls and joined in their screams, even falling on the floor once to shake all over. I felt none of the sensations I had felt before. My mind did not let itself be taken over now. Now my accusations were part of a carefully made scheme. Just before I followed Mistress Putnam from the church, I glanced back to look at Mercy Lewis again. Would she help me?

Chapter Seventeen

After Gabe's hearing I was allowed to roam freely again. On a day when Mistress Putnam and Ann were both busy at the Parrises', I made my way to Mary Putnam's house.

"You are not welcome here," she said when I knocked at the door, and she pulled her small body up to look strong.

"Please," I said. "I have thought of a plan that might save Gabe and others. My plan made it necessary to cry out against him in court."

She looked at me for a long moment. I could see that her face had aged, and there was sadness in her green eyes. "Come in," she said at last.

Two surprises waited for me inside. Joseph Putnam was there, and so was Roger, Rebecca Nurse's parrot. The bird cried out, "Hello there!"

"Gabe went to get him when Rebecca was arrested." Her voice broke. "Sometimes even now I cannot believe what has happened. To know that Rebecca, such a dear, dear soul . . ." She stopped talking and Joseph came to put his arm around her shoulders and led her to a rocking chair.

At once I began to tell them my plan. Joseph Putnam was doubtful at first, but gradually he changed his mind. "It might work," he said. "I wish you could try your plot at once, but I believe more time is needed, more time for you to gain the girls' trust again and for the climate of the leaders to soften. Already I have heard that Reverend Increase Mather is worried that innocent people could be convicted."

When I bade them good-bye, Goody Putnam hugged me.

"I will find a way to get into the jail to see Gabe," said Joseph. "I want to give him hope." He shook his head. "I boasted once that I would not see anyone of my household touched by this ungodly business, but now I have. More guards are kept at the prison now. There is no possibility of getting the boy out, but mayhap I can bribe one of the men to let me in."

"Oh." I clasped my hands as if in prayer. "I so want him to know I am trying, and please tell him I never thought him guilty. Please tell him I would rather die than see him hanged."

"Come to me when you are ready," called Mary Putnam as I walked away from her door. "You are welcome here."

The summer days that followed seemed longer and longer. I went to hearings and trials, always ready to scream accusations and to pretend to suffer the injuries of witchcraft. Salem Prison was bursting at the seams with those waiting for trials or for execution. Prisoners were being sent to private jailers, who were paid to chain them in barns or sheds. I reminded myself constantly that Gabe would soon be tried. I had to do my part. I had to be a star among the afflicted girls, had to be trusted by all those engaged in the witch hunt.

I even attended hangings, and although desperately sick to my stomach, I applauded when the bodies swung from the ladder. It was at Mary Easty's execution that I had a brief moment alone with Mercy Lewis. She stood by herself slightly apart from the others, and I went to stand beside her.

Her face looked strained, and I decided to risk everything by being truthful with her. "It makes me ill," I said softly, and a great shudder passed through my body. "How horrible to watch so fine a woman come to this end."

Mercy turned quickly toward me. "You'd best keep such words to yourself," she said, "else you will find yourself in Salem Prison, and I can tell you it is not a pleasant place."

I reached for her hand. "Mercy," I said, "forgive me for being afraid to stand with you. I was afraid for Gabe and for myself." I shook my head. "Had I been as brave as you were, had there been two of us." I shrugged. "Mayhap someone would have listened had there been two of us."

"Why do you say these things now?"

"Because I am ready to do what is right." I swallowed hard. "I have a plan to save Gabe, and others. I hope you will help me."

"Oh, no." She shook her head vigorously. "I know not what you are thinking to do, but I know I want no part of it."

"Just listen to me, please," I said, and I told her then all I had worked out in my mind, told it quickly and with my heart laid out for her to see. When my words had all tumbled forth, I held my breath, waiting, and I looked at her.

Finally, she nodded her head. "I'll do it," she said. "May God help us!"

"He will," I said. "This madness must be stopped."

We knew that a hanging was scheduled two days hence, and we decided it would be a good occasion for our efforts. The timing turned out to be better than we could have ever hoped for. That morning four ministers arrived from outside the village. They traveled each on his own horse, but riding together, and wearing their Sunday robes. They came to attend the hanging of one of their own, George Burroughs.

I spied them as they stopped in front of the Parrises' house, and I called to Mistress Putnam to come and look. I recognized

Reverend John Hale from nearby Beverly and Reverend Nicholas Noyes from Salem Town, who had come to pray for Betty and Abigail. Of course, I also knew our former minister Deodat Lawson. The last man to dismount was familiar, too. "There is Cotton Mather. He has come again to Salem Village, and him the second most important minister in Massachusetts. Only his father, Increase Mather, is more respected." Delight shot through me, and only by great effort did I stop myself from clapping. Cotton Mather had been part of my plan from the beginning, but I had not expected for the man to be present when I worked my magic.

As we drove to Gallows Hill, I prayed and I hoped. This was my one and only chance to save Gabe. Every mile we traveled seemed like a thousand. Ann poked me in the side with her elbow. "Why do you keep your eyes closed?" she demanded.

I opened them long enough to look at her once. "I am praying," I said. "I hope you've no objection to prayer." I closed my eyes again. She said nothing, but I heard her make a small huffing sound.

At Gallows Hill we stayed in the carriage. "We can see well from here," Mistress Putnam declared. "We may as well be comfortable."

When the ministers appeared, people cheered. They rode to the front of the crowd and dismounted. Just before George Burroughs was forced up the ladder, he spoke. He said that he would die praying that the evil that had caused the death of innocent people in Salem Village would be stopped. Then in a clear strong voice he recited the Lord's Prayer.

The crowd began to murmur and move about. Was it not true that no witch could recite the prayer? Could this man have been wrongly convicted? I hoped someone would push forward and start the movement to free him, but Reverend Cotton Mather mounted his horse, stood tall in the stirrups, and shouted. He said that Satan had become more clever because Salem's Godly warriors were about to defeat him. He called out that the hanging must proceed, and it did.

I had, by this time, seen many people hanged. Each time I looked away and tried not to think of the body swinging just at the corner of my eye. This time was different. I looked full at Reverend Burroughs. I looked, and I remembered his kindness to his daughter, and how gentle were his prayers. I did something else, too. I made a promise. While I looked at his body, I promised to do all I could to stop this senseless waste of human life, and it was time for me to take action.

I stood and screamed. "No, no, Mistress Mather!" I shouted. "Do not hurt me more. Have I not told you that I would not sign that horrible book?!" I put my arms up as if to ward off blows.

Mercy, true to her word, picked up on my lead. "Lady Phips is with Mistress Mather. Do you not see them?" She pointed upward. "They ride about us on brooms!"

"Lady Phips!" I screamed. "I care not that you are the governor's wife! I will never give my soul to Satan! Strike me as you will, I will never sign your foul book!" I planned next to fall back on the carriage seat in a sort of fit, but that was unnecessary.

Young Ann did not like being left out of the limelight. She stood, issued a scream of terror, and put her arms about her own neck as if to protect it. "Mistress Mather!" she yelled, "please do not cut my throat!"

Abigail Williams and Mary Warren were next to cry out that Mistress Mather and Lady Phips were tormenting them. Two or three other girls joined in.

Cotton Mather was still in the saddle. For a moment he stared in our direction, then rode toward our carriage. "Madam!" he shouted to Mistress Putnam. "This is ridiculous. You must control your children."

"Lady Phips!" I shrieked. "Governor's wife or not, I will not join your coven!"

"Drucilla," said Mistress Putnam, but I ignored her and struck at the air.

"This crowd should disperse at once," commanded Cotton Mather, and he began to ride about waving his arms in a shooing sort of motion.

Mistress Putnam was furious with me. "Be quiet!" she yelled, but I kept up the shouts about the governor's wife and Mistress Mather until Thomas Putnam had driven the buggy away from Gallows Hill. No one spoke on the drive. When we were inside the kitchen, Mistress Putnam grabbed my arm. "You have most likely ruined everything!"

"Good," I said, "such was my intention."

She slapped me hard. I think she would have continued to do so had not Thomas Putnam stepped behind her and held her arm when she raised it again. "It's over, Ann," he said. "It's finally over."

I had my mother's miniature in my pocket, and I had earlier hidden Gabe's plaque and Thomas's star. I would get them as I walked through the woods, and I wanted nothing more from the house. With Thomas still holding his wife, I hurried out the back door. I regretted only that I knew young Thomas and Elizabeth would miss me. I would miss them as well. I turned to look back at the house just once before I started through the fields toward Mary Putnam's.

Two days later it was all over. Word came from Boston that Governor Phips had forbidden any more witch trials where only spectral evidence was used. There would be no more hangings of those convicted on such evidence. It did not happen all at once, but gradually forty-nine prisoners were released from prison.

Even still, the prisoners were required to pay for their food and lodging while in prison.

Gabe was not among the first to be released, and although I hated the idea that he should spend one more night in that horrible prison, I was, in a way, glad. I wanted to be gone before he came. "He will want to see you," Mary Putnam said. "You know Joseph was able to get word to him about what you did to stop all the madness." I only shook my head. I had no words to explain my great need to be away from Salem Village and even from Gabe.

We sat slicing apples for drying. Autumn had begun to paint the leaves outside the kitchen window with bright colors. I was surprised to realize that October was almost come. The spring and summer had gone by in a blur while I was lost in the witch frenzy. "I long to go across the ocean," I told her, "but I suppose I must settle for Salem Town."

"I have a friend in Salem Town, one of my neighbors when I lived there. Marie is French, but she married a man from England. Neither family could accept the marriage because of differences in religion, so Marie and William came to this country, where he made a great deal of money in shipping. William died a few months ago, and I have heard that Marie plans to go back to France soon. She wants to use her money to establish a school, a home really, for orphans in Paris."

I sucked in my breath. Was I told this story for a reason? "Oh, how I long to be a part of such an effort." I left my place on the kitchen bench and knelt beside Goody Putnam. "I know I am undeserving, but still I cannot but hope. Is there any chance I might be able to go with your friend?"

And so in less than a fortnight, I would be boarding a ship for France. Gabe was released from prison while I stayed with Marie Hall as we made preparations for our journey. It was I who opened her door one night when he knocked. "Oh," I said, and I stepped back.

He reached out to hold my arm. "Don't run from me, Dru," he said gently. "I am not angry with you." He was thinner than I had ever seen him, and I saw a scar at the edge of his sleeve. I wondered if his arms had been chained as well as his legs.

"But I am angry with myself," I said. "I need time, and I need work. Mayhap scrubbing floors and washing clothes will help cleanse my spirit." I touched his dear cheek. "I must have time and distance away from the vile air of Salem Village if I hope to find forgiveness."

He took my hand. "Try writing it down, Dru," he said. "I will send you a book. Recording it may help you see that you, too, were a victim. You can keep the book, and if one of our children should hear of what happened someday, mayhap you will let him read his mother's story."

I could not speak, but I squeezed his hand. Gabe put his arms about me when we parted, and he kissed me. I loved being close to him, but feeling undeserving, I pulled away quickly.

Two days later a delivery came for me from a Salem Town shop. I held the brown book in my hand and breathed in the scent of the leather binding. On the first page I read, "For Round Hair, fill these pages, and come back to me soon, Gabe."

Mistress Hall and I traveled to Boston and there boarded a huge vessel bound for France. On the morning we left, I felt better than I had on any day since the time of the witches began. As the ship moved out to sea, I looked at the Boston shore, but what I saw was Salem Village. Thomas Putnam's home, the parsonage, the meeting house, Ingersoll's Ordinary, Rebecca Nurse's home, they all flashed through my mind. I saw them against the backdrop of a bare and frozen landscape. I knew I had surely seen some beauty in that dark village. Surely there had been springtime and blossoms, yet none could be found in my memory, only desolate roads and stark buildings.

On the long voyage, I have spent a good deal of time on the deck, staring out at the endless water. The weather has grown quite cold, and I have been often urged to go below. I have wrapped myself against the cold and stayed at the railing. About halfway through the journey I felt ready to tell this story. Now before I can begin my work in France, I need to explain myself to the man I have left behind.

Dear Gabe,

As I take pen in hand, I am still at sea. I know you are at Harvard College by now. I can picture you there in a room that is full of books, and I am certain you touch the pages like a mother touches her infant. Thinking of you among your books makes me smile, and I find smiles most difficult to come by these days.

You were right to tell me to record the story of the great darkness that came upon Salem Village and upon my soul. The writing sorted out for me the facts and the progression of the disease that enveloped me and so many others. There will always be sorrow in my heart for what I have done, but I do now feel hope that I might be able to forgive myself.

Madame Hall is teaching me French, so I will be able to communicate with the children who come to us. I look forward to meeting those young ones who have been orphaned just as you and I were, but even more I look forward to hours and days of physical labor. For some reason, I believe strongly that hard, hard work will make me free.

Thank you, my dear Gabe, for being always a light in the black night. We will soon reach land, and I will post this letter. Someday, when the gloom has been driven from me, I will come back to America and to you.

With all my love,
Drucilla

Author's Note

I have always been interested in the Salem witch trials, and I became even more fascinated while doing research for this book. Although my Drucilla and Gabe are totally fictional characters, almost everyone else in the story really did live. What made the girls do what they did? Authorities disagree. Some think it was all for fun, some think the whole thing began with greed and revenge, some think it was an example of mass hysteria. A recent theory even proposes it was caused by ergot poisoning from a crop of fungus-infected rye, which led to hallucinations.

While I was in college, two girls who lived across the hall played a joke on my roommate and me. They sneaked into our room and arranged chocolate sprinkles, made for cake decoration, around the room as if a rat had deposited them. This happened twice. The horrified dorm mother picked up a dropping with a tissue and planned to have it analyzed in the science lab to discover what creature had visited us. When she announced we would have to move to another room, our friends confessed. My reason for telling this story is that I was certain I saw the rat under my bed. Since that day, I have known that my mind is very susceptible to the power of suggestion. I am afraid that had I been a girl in Salem in 1692 I might well have thought myself afflicted by witches.

The division in the Putnam family was real, and definitely did play a part in the witch hunt. Joseph Putnam was an outspoken opponent of the trials and really did threaten his sister-in-law not to accuse anyone belonging to his immediate family. Joseph was the father of Israel Putnam, who became a famous general during the Revolutionary War. The church's division over Reverend Samuel Parris and his demands was also real. Ann Putnam, the older, was at the heart of the accusations and she, along with a few other adults, also claimed to be tormented by the witches.

Ann Putnam, the daughter, and Abigail Williams, the minister's niece, were younger than the other girls, but they seemed to be the leaders among the afflicted girls. It is true that one girl admitted she had lied, and she really was accused, then, of being a witch herself. She repented and went back to being an accuser. I found it interesting that Ann Putnam was the only one of the girls to publicly apologize for what she did. In 1706, she asked the church to forgive her. Her mother and father had been dead a few years by that time.

Nineteen people were hanged as witches in Salem. George Burroughs, the former Salem Village minister, was one of them. Giles Cory was really pressed to death, and four other people died in prison waiting for trials. I visited the towns of Salem and Danvers, once called Salem Village. I was moved by the sight of Rebecca Nurse's home and the site of her burial. Her sister Mary Easty really did write a touching letter to the judges, not begging for her own life to be spared, but asking that the trials be stopped to spare other innocent people.

Eventually some ministers, not involved in the trials, began to doubt the truth of the accusations. After several prominent people, including the governor's wife, had been accused, Governor

Phips declared that no more spectral evidence could be used in court. People could no longer be tried on evidence that could not be seen by everyone. Close to 150 people had been arrested, and the jails were full. Those people were not released until they had paid for their prison food and lodging. In order to pay her bill, Samuel Parris sold Tituba to another slave holder.

In 1992, three hundred years after the trials, Massachusetts lawmakers passed a resolution officially stating that those accused of witchcraft had really been innocent. That same year a beautiful memorial was erected. It lists the names of all who died and records some of the brave words uttered by the innocent. It stands across the street from the site of the original meeting-house and is a reminder that we must be advocates for tolerance and slow to accuse.

THE DEAD

NINETEEN ACCUSED WITCHES WERE HANGED ON GALLOWS HILL IN 1692:

JUNE 10

Bridget Bishop

JULY 19

Rebecca Nurse • Sarah Good • Susannah Martin
Elizabeth Howe • Sarah Wildes

AUGUST 19

George Burroughs • Martha Carrier • John Willard
George Jacobs, Sr. • John Proctor

SEPTEMBER 22

Martha Corey • Mary Easty • Ann Pudeator
Alice Parker • Mary Parker • Wilmott Redd
Margaret Scott • Samuel Wardell

ONE ACCUSED WITCH WAS PRESSED TO DEATH:

SEPTEMBER 19

Giles Corey

OTHER ACCUSED WITCHES DIED IN PRISON:

Sarah Osborne • Roger Toothaker
Lyndia Dustin • Ann Foster

As many as thirteen others may have died in prison.*

*Sources conflict with the exact number of prison deaths.